The Lost Voyage
by
Shawn Shallow

Characters

Ship's Crew
Joseph Baines - Sailmaker
Arthur Conan Doyle - Medical Officer & Harpooner
James Garret - Captain
Li Jun - Cook
Silas Lentz - First Harpooner
Robert MacLeod - Chief Boatswain Mate
Richard Moore - Storekeeper
Carter Winthrop - Midshipman

Other Characters
Alistair Cross - Chemist (pharmacist)
Elijah Grantham - Seminary Professor
Edwin Mulligan - Detective Sergeant
Madame Seraphine - Medium

4

Preface
The Derelict
Arctic 1878

The whaleboat cut silently through the Arctic water, its oars dipping with a slow, rhythmic creak. Above, the waning sun was a dim blur, barely visible through the shifting mist, casting a glow over the scene. It felt as if they were rowing into another world, a place where time had been forgotten.

Doyle's athletic body sat erect, a wool cap covering his brown hair - atop a mustached face. His contrasting gray eyes peered intently into the dense fog trying to make out the looming silhouette of the derelict ship.

The *Octavius*, as it was named, had appeared like a phantom on the edge of the floating sea ice, its dark hull barely discernible through the haze. There had been no movement on deck, no sign of life. Now, as they rowed closer, the oppressive silence deepened, broken only by the soft splash of oars and the occasional groan of wood from the whale ship *Herald*'s crew as they pulled through the water.

"Give it a hail," Captain Garret grunted, his voice low, strained with unease. "Let them know we're comin'."

"Aye," replied Chief Boatswains Mate MacLeod, glancing nervously into the fog. He stood up, cupping his hands to his mouth as he called out into the mist. "Ahoy there!" His voice echoed faintly, the sound quickly swallowed by the fog, leaving only the low murmur of the water lapping against the the rowboat. There was no answer.

The sailors exchanged uneasy glances. Doyle felt a shiver run down his spine, though whether from the cold or something deeper, he couldn't say.

"Maybe they didn't hear us," MacLeod muttered, his voice barely above a whisper. "Or maybe..." He trailed off, glancing toward Captain Garret, but said nothing more.

An unspoken fear hung in the air, thick as the mist around them. Doyle remained silent, his eyes fixed ahead, where the dark shape of the ship slowly grew larger in the mist. The whaleboat oars dipped again, cutting the water with a slow, steady rhythm. Each stroke seemed to carry them closer to the outline of the ship looming ahead. The eerie quiet pressed in from all sides, making every sound seem louder, every breath more strained.

"Ahoy there!" MacLeod yelled again.

Still, there was no response. The rowers pulled again, the oars dragging as if the sea itself resisted their progress. The derelict *Octavius* was close now, adrift in the Arctic fog. On closer inspection, the ship's hull was weathered and slick with ice, its sides encrusted with frost that glittered faintly in the dim light. Frost clung to its masts and heavily damaged sails hung limp like the tattered remnants of some forgotten era. It was eerily still. No lights flickered on board, no voices called out to greet them. The ship looked dead.

The whaleboat bumped softly against the ship's hull, the hollow thud reverberating through the silence. The sailors secured their oars, staring up at the ship with wide eyes, their breaths coming in shallow puffs. For a long moment, no one spoke. Doyle felt a tight knot of dread forming in his chest as he peered up at the deck.

"Something's not right," Captain Garret muttered.

Doyle nodded, though he said nothing. He couldn't shake the feeling that they were intruding on something long dead, something that should have been left undisturbed.

"Best get aboard and see what's what," said the Captain.

One by one, the men began climbing the frozen rigging that dangled down the sides. Doyle was the last to follow, his hands stiff from the cold as he gripped the icy ropes. The boat below rocked making the climb more difficult. As Doyle hoisted himself, he felt as though they were being watched — by whom or what, he couldn't say.

As Doyle reached the rail and hauled himself over the gunwale, the boat crew stood in silence. The only sound was the creak of the ship's frozen deck beneath their boots, and the wind weaving through the rigging like a wail. The *Octavius* offered no welcome. Only silence and a long dead dead crew at their posts.

England 1900
(the present)

Chapter
Haunting Invitation

The rhythmic clattering of train wheels against iron tracks resonated with a comforting cadence, drowning-out the lingering echoes of Doyle's thoughts. He sat in a first-class compartment with a bird's eye view of the lush English countryside. However, the picturesque view went unnoticed as his mind wandered to memories of a time when he called the sea home. The train plodded toward the coastal town of Whitby where the aged whaling ship *Herald* lay docked awaiting its final trip to the scrapyard.

Doyle's fingers absentmindedly traced the neatly penned script of the invitation recently received. The letter arrived just days prior in the familiar handwriting of Captain James Garret, the *Herald's* former master. But Garret's words seemed uncharacteristic and beckoned for Doyle to visit his former ship.

Dear Dr. Doyle,

I hope this letter finds you well. I write to extend an invitation that may stir ghosts from our past. I believe it is time for us to gather once more aboard the Herald, for there are matters left unsaid, and shadows that must be confronted. Join your shipmates before her final retiring voyage.

The letter continued with a location and date for which to meet. The location was none other than the old ship where his former shipmates waited along with a paranormal medium. Doyle's brow furrowed as he reread the letter. Being drawn back to the ship and the strange event they narrowly survived was unwelcome. The addition of a 'so called' medium added an additional level of discomfort. However, given the nature of the event they would revisit, a medium was not entirely out of place.

The letter also promised the former crew £100 sterling for their attendance - presumably from the sale of *Herald* to the scrapyard. That amount could easily buy a modest country cottage for a weary sailor. Doyle himself was both a successful author *and* physician, not lacking in wealth, so the funds weren't a reason for attendance. His reason went much deeper.

Seances, and mediums had recently become fashionable and even the source of organized entertainment. These spiritual guides plied their wares in private parlors and public halls alike. The scene was always the same. The medium would sit at a table in a dimly lit room or public stage, the air heavy with anticipation. Soon, the voices of lost loved ones, supposedly channeled from the world beyond, would be heard along with aberrations like moving objects or eerie knocking. Attendees even reported changes in temperature, gusts of air, or the translucent presence of ghostly specters.

As the creator of a literary detective, Doyle was often invited to discern the authenticity of the spiritualist. Unlike his fictional detective, Doyle had no amazing powers of observation or blistering intellect. As a result, he struggled to prove, or disprove, their authenticity.

In frustration, he frequently turned to medical colleagues for a metaphysical view, only to find more confusion. Some physicians believed that the paranormal had a bonafide role in human health and speculated that a patient's "unseen ailments" such as "hysteria" were actually attributed to a spiritual imbalance or possession. Others even prescribed the use of a medium to administer treatment in the form of a seance. At the end of the day, Doyle found himself a skeptical believer, haunted by the possibility that there might be something more.

Unfortunately, as his fame as the creator of Holmes spread, he was invited to investigate reports of the supernatural with increasing frequency. One of these instances involved two young girls from Cottingley, England. The youths had taken a series of photographs that showed them playing with fairies in their garden. The photographs were striking, ethereal images that captured the imagination of the public. Doyle arranged for a professional photographer to examine the photos and the setting in which they were taken. The photographer declared them to be authentic. Doyle presented these findings in the *The Strand Magazine* declaring proof that the mystical world and fairies were real. Soon, journalists and skeptics began to poke holes in the story. "The fairies," they said, "looked too much like paper cutouts." In fact, the fairies were traced back to a popular children's book. Despite headlines branding Doyle gullible, he continued in his assertion that the Cottingley Fairies were real.

Sighing, Doyle rose from his seat, the weight of the past heavy on his shoulders. Despite the controversy, he never discussed the origin of his spiritual beliefs from the voyage 20 years earlier.

Chapter
Arrival at the Reunion

As the train rounded a bend, a breathtaking view of the ocean was revealed. The sea met the sky in a dazzling blend of blues and grays. Doyle leaned out the window inhaling the salty air. He could almost hear the call of the ocean, its rhythmic waves echoing the heartbeat of the very vessel he was about to revisit.

As the train drew closer to the final station, Doyle felt a wave of mixed emotion. The events of his first voyage meant that some of his shipmates would meet him with open arms, while another wouldn't meet him at all. After this recollection, he closed the window and returned to his seat The air inside the compartment grew heavy, but the train's whistle pulled him from his reverie. Doyle shifted in his seat, his mind racing with questions. *What had finally compelled Captain Garret to summon everyone together? What truths could he possibly unearth on the decaying ship after all this time?*

The train screeched to a halt at Whitby station signaling Doyle to gather his belongings. He stepped onto the platform where the salty breeze granted some new comfort. The sea scent mixed with the earthy aroma of the nearby moors, ignited a spark of wonder not felt since his initial voyage. The station was bustling with travelers, but Doyle quickly felt a sense of isolation. He moved with purpose toward the docks where the distant silhouette of *Herald* cut through the horizon. As he approached the docks, the sight of the well worn ship made him feel all his years. The once-majestic vessel stood in disrepair, her hull marred by years of pounding sea ice.

"Ahoy there, Doyle," called Captain Garret from above on the ship's railing. His face was was equally weathered by time and the sea as if locked into the same fate as the *Herald*. Doyle met his gaze, a mixture of warmth and apprehension flooding his senses. The captain's expression was likewise mixed as if he tried to hide a great burden behind a forced smile.

Doyle respected Garret who embodied a seasoned mariner. Born into a family of seamen, Garret was reared on a ship as a cabin boy. He quickly rose through the ranks of various ships to ultimately take command of the *Herald*. Every ounce of his experience was needed to command the whaler in the tumultuous waters of the Arctic Ocean. Now two decades later, Garret stood watching his beloved ship awaiting its final trip to the scrapyard. The moment wasn't lost on Doyle who would like nothing better than to provide badly needed closure to the events of 20 years earlier.

"Skipper," Doyle replied, stepping onto the gangplank. "It's good to see you again, though I wish it were under happier circumstances."

"True enough," replied the captain. "But for now, let's get reacquainted with your old shipmates."

With a sense of foreboding, Doyle followed Garret onto the ship, the wooden deck creaking beneath their weight. The atmosphere was thick with memories as he descended into the ship's familiar interior seemingly frozen in time.

Doyle and the captain made their way to the galley. The ship was a hollow shell of its former self—anchored in the harbor, waiting to be broken down for scrap. Doyle, now an older man with the beginnings of gray streaks in his brown hair couldn't help but reflect on the crew he'd known so well. Doyle's eyes adjusted to the small room illuminated by a single porthole on opposite bulkheads of whitewashed wood. It contained the original three tables used during his voyage for everything from eating to card games. Each table was rectangular with benches on either side that could accommodate up to three men. However, the normal crew compliment was an even dozen. Following the many years since his time on the *Herald*, only seven men remained for the reunion.

Standing nearest Doyle was Li Jun, the Chinese cook. Li was short, but stood erect with a silent confidence. He never spoke of his past, leading the crew to ascribe this regal bearing to a fanciful past. They conjectured occupations from former Shaolin priest, to a nobleman on the run from deadly palace intrigue. Li typically occupied the compact kitchen adjoining the galley where he served food from a small window. When not serving, Li was typically found preparing for the next meal chopping vegetables for a pot of stew or making dough for johnny cakes, both daily stables. The sailors ate the biscuit cakes alone, with fish caught that day, or dipped in a stew to extract every drop of broth. Li was short and generally quiet unless provoked by the crew's complaints. After chastised beyond his patience, he would launch into a borage of Chinese insults. His pantry contained unique asian herbs and spices that drew Doyle's curiosity. Li spent occasional leisure describing those with medicinal application to Doyle who took notes.

In the opposite corner sat Joseph Baines, sailmaker. Baines was a pudgy man with rounded shoulders from years crouched over canvas in need of repair. He had a certain peace about him, despite harsh sea conditions. While others complained of the cold or endless tasks, Baines would simply sit, needle in hand, fixing what needed fixing. Baines likewise never spoke of his life -

mainly due to lack of a family. However, given his dull appearance and natural introversion, his past was never the subject of conjecture. Baines simply existed as part of the background like a portrait.

In contrast to Baine's quiet demeanor was Midshipman Carter Winthrop. Winthrop was the spoiled child of the ship's owner - sent aboard the *Herald* to 'learn the trade.' He talked incessantly about his family or elite boarding school friends, much to the annoyance of everyone within earshot. At average height, the red haired and freckled Winthrop, though a lowly midshipman, would strut through the *Herald* as if he owned the place. Doyle heard in the years following their voyage that Winthrop's father died unexpectedly, leaving Winthrop the estate. However, he quickly squandered the family fortune and sold the shipping company to cover his debts. At a glance, the change in fortune didn't seem to humble Winthrop who complained about the quality of the hired coach delivering him to the reunion. His rant was punctuated by the tapping of a stylish walking cane astride a flamboyant suit of the latest style. Doyle wondered if Winthrop's attire represented the last remnants of the family estate, or were borrowed specifically for the occasion.

Sitting at a table alone was the decrepit looking Richard Moore, storekeeper. If Doyle had guessed in advance who would be sitting alone at this reunion, it was Moore. Even two decades prior, Moore had the mannerisms associated with an old curmudgeon. He had been in charge of the ship's provisions and the subject of crew grumbling about tainted water and substandard meat. On more than one occasion, a barrel would be opened to find old canvas as filler among the food within which Moore blamed on an merchant from the last port. More than one crewman surmised that Moore had been skimming funds and sharing the proceeds with unscrupulous suppliers of his dubious acquaintance. His wife was said to have left him for one such man.

"I'm surprised you dandies had time for the likes of us," said Robert MacLeod, the ship's chief boatswain's mate. Doyle recoiled at the guttural voice. MacLeod was always a man with aggressive mannerisms. Now, 20 years later, his rugged frame was replaced by that of a man accustomed to living on a barstool. A gray beard and unkempt hair stood atop an unsteady body holding a spent cigar. However, MacLeod's personality seemed unchanged as reflected by the careless use of the word 'dandy" which referred to men only focused on fashion. Doyle had always assumed that MacLeod's disdain for Doyle personally was linked to MacLeod's childhood home in the Clearances of the Scottish Highlands. The Clearances were the tenements of last resort for the poorest of families. In contrast, Doyle's family lived in a comfortable bungalow paid for by his father's modest civil service position. Doyle having attended the University of Edinburgh only added to the separation.

"Thank you for your kind presence," interjected Captain Garrett through gritted teeth, now standing beside Doyle.

"If you had listened to me 20 years ago, we may have avoided this little party," retorted MacLeod.

The interchange would have turned into an argument had it not been for the entrance of Madame Seraphine. It was said that she communed with the dead, but her appearance looked anything but deceased. Her beauty was striking; her long black hair fell in waves over her shoulders, shimmering in the light like the midnight sea. Her eyes, deep pools of midnight blue, sparkled with a peculiar intensity that seemed to see right through any onlooker.

She wore a flowing gown of deep green, the fabric clinging to her figure.

"Good afternoon, gentlemen," she said, her voice smooth and melodic. "I trust I'm not interrupting anything."

Doyle paused, slightly stunned. He had done a preliminary investigation of the spiritualist and heard of her stage presence. His investigation also found that the enigmatic Seraphine had seemingly appeared out of thin air with no trace of a previous history. Her sudden rise to fame began on the London stage where she captivated audiences with her dramatic flair and mysterious persona.

Her debut performance in *The Shadow's Embrace* was a dark and haunting tragedy that became an overnight success. Seraphine played the role of a noblewoman haunted by visions of her dead lover. Her performance was so convincing that rumors swirled about her connection to the supernatural. Critics praised her as a revelation, though whispers in the theater district hinted that she was more than just an actress.

Following *The Shadow's Embrace*, she starred in *Midnight at Blackmoor Hall*, a gothic melodrama about a cursed estate. Her portrayal of a tormented heiress on the verge of madness solidified her reputation as a master of the macabre. She seemed to embody her characters with an intensity that unsettled even the most hardened theatergoers.

Shortly thereafter, she was invited to private high society residences to conduct seances. These mystic evenings, in combination with her stage reputation, cemented her credentials with the paranormal. Despite his best efforts, Doyle could find no records of her existence prior to her sudden rise to prominence. No birth certificate, no family, no acquaintances from her past. It was as if Madame Seraphine had materialized from nothing — just like the ghostly figures with which she communed. The bigger question was *why here and now*? A small gathering on an old ship was hardly the venue for the great Madama Seraphine who commanded large audiences and even larger sums of money. Doyle wondered... *is she here to advance her fame by debunking the creator of the popular literary detective Sherlock S. Holmes?*

Doyle stepped forward. "Madame Seraphine, I presume?"

"You presume correctly, Dr. Doyle," she replied cooly.

Her beauty in such close proximity left Doyle slightly stunned. In response, he took a single step back and attempted to turn into the detached character of Holmes. "Your arrival has stirred a fair bit of excitement among my associates. How did you come to be at our humble gathering?"

She met his gaze, unflinching. "The spirits are drawn to those who seek them with sincere hearts, Dr. Doyle. They wish to communicate with their loved ones - to share their truths. They deserve peace do they not? I'm here to give it to them."

Doyle furrowed his brow. "I was referring to the identity of a more *temporal* host, Madame."

"I'm not at liberty to reveal the *temporal* source, Dr. Doyle," she said coyly. "However, I believe they were acting upon the needs of a *less-temporal* benefactor."

"I see," replied Doyle with masked irritation. "Would you care to identify the *less-temporal* benefactor then?

Seraphine smiled, "I believe it would be better to let them identify themself at the appropriate time."

"I assume that time would be at a seance of your control," said Doyle with a contrived smile.

Now it was Seraphine who flashed a masked annoyance. She then collected herself with a grin and replied, "If you're implying that I'm a charlatan, you are mistaken. However, I'm sure we're in agreement that souls must be put to rest by any means possible. You're certainly invited to conduct your your own empirical investigation without protest, no matter where it might lead…"

Doyle would have expected theatrics, perhaps even a spirited display of disdain for a non-believer, that was the usual formula used by the so called 'mystics'. However, Madame Seraphine's controlled discipline and invitation for scrutiny was unexpected. There was more to this woman that met the eye.

MacLeod stepped forward. "I put my money on the great beyond instead of your earthly investigation, Doyle. It's you that brought these spirits among us anyway."

"Enough," said Captain Garret defaulting to the manner of speech of a lifelong mariner. "If we're t' uncover the truth, we all got t' work together," Garret said firmly. "The answer might lie in the hands o' spirits, or in the hands o' men. Either way, by thunder, we'll see this through 'fore the *Herald* meets her end."

Doyle stood silent for a moment. "Very well, Madame. You take the lead and be our guide. I'm looking forward to seeing these abilities I've heard so much about."

"And you, Dr. Doyle. Please demonstrate the skills you've carefully endowed in your character of Sherlock S. Holmes. I, for one, truly hope they are engrained in their creator," she said with curious sincerity. "We will begin at tomorrow evening in this very room."

After a few pleasantries, each crewman retreated to his respective quarters on the *Herald* while Madama Seraphine withdrew to a local inn. Doyle removed himself to peer at the night sky not unlike the heavenly scenes of his first voyage.

Arctic 1878
(20 years earlier)

Chapter
Birth of a Sailor

Doyle was in need of money - badly in need. Edinburgh's medical college didn't come cheap and he required funds to finish his medical studies. He'd heard that whaling ships offered substantial pay for common seamen—enough to cover a year's tuition. As a result, Doyle soon found himself on route to Leith, where the whaling ship *Herald* lay at anchor.

The ship was a formidable sight, her sturdy frame and towering masts rising against the gray sky in preparation for the Arctic fishing grounds. A gruff voice broke his reverie. "Ye lookin' to sign on?"

Doyle turned to see a stocky man with a neatly cropped beard and piercing dark eyes. He had the look of a man who had spent his life at sea.

"Yes, Sir," Doyle said, squaring his shoulders. "I've heard you're looking for crew. I'm a medical student, half-finished with my studies."

Captain Garrett eyed him with suspicion. "I've no need, we do our own doctoring. You have the look of an athlete, though. How might you be with a harpoon?"

When Doyle wasn't in the classroom, he was generally found on the sports field. The captain recognized his muscular frame and rugged appearance topped by a square jaw. "I can master it - I've no doubt," said Doyle with an air of confidence that came with his natural competitiveness. "I've got strong arms and a steady hand."

The captain considered him for a moment, then grunted. "Fair enough. We've lost men to sickness and worse on these voyages. Could use someone to do both. The Arctic seas are unforgiving, and whaling's not for the weak-hearted. We sail tomorrow. Be here at dawn if ye're still keen."

It was in this way that Doyle found himself on the bustling deck of the *Herald* struggling to stay out of the crew's way as they prepared to get underway. The sailors hauled on lines, prepared heavy sails and shouted orders across the deck. The anchor, dripping with seawater, was winched up, clanking against the hull as the ship groaned into motion. A stiff wind filled the canvas, and the *Herald* began to shift in the water, breaking free from the dock.

Doyle felt a little lost amidst the frenetic energy. The crew moved like clockwork, each knowing his role. His task was supposed to be that of a ship's doctor, but at this moment, he felt more like a visitor than a working member of the crew.

"All hands, tighten the trim!" shouted Captain Garret from the quarterdeck. The sailors responded instantly, hauling on the lines, muscles straining as they maneuvered the sails into place. Doyle watched the scene, but his respite from work didn't last long.

"Lookin' a bit lost, eh?" a voice said from behind him.

Doyle turned to see a young man, tall and muscular, with sun-beaten skin and an easy smile. He was in his early twenties but carried himself with the confidence of someone who had spent more than a decade at sea. His bright blue eyes were sharp, a mix of humor and experience.

"Name's Silas," the man had said, extending a hand. "Harpooner on the *Herald*. Been a sailor since I was twelve."

Doyle took his hand, feeling the strength in his grip. "Doyle, first voyage."

Silas chuckled. "I figured as much. Captain told me you were comin'. Said you looked athletic and sharp. That's why you're not just playin' doctor on this ship."

Silas picked up a nearby harpoon and handed it to him. The metal head was heavy in Doyle's hands, its sharp point gleaming in the sun. "This," Silas said, tapping the barbed tip, "is what you'll be throwin' when we're out there chasin' whales. You'll be in-charge of the second boat. The other fella got himself injured."

Doyle's heart quickened. "But I've never…"

Silas laughed. "Ain't many men get that responsibility on their first time out, but the captain has a feeling about you. Your main job on this ship is gonna be as a harpooner, patchin' up the crew comes as needed. When you're leadin' the second boat, the lads will be rowin' like hades to get close to a whale. When we're close enough, it's up to you to hook the big fish."

Doyle looked at the harpoon again, the weight of it suddenly feeling heavier in his hands. "And if I miss?"

Silas shrugged with a grin. "Well, then we've got a bit of a problem…but you won't. The whale's a big target, and we'll get you close. Just remember—it's not just about strength, it's about accuracy and timing. The whale won't sit still, so you've got to make your move at the right moment."

Doyle nodded, trying to absorb the information.

Silas repositioned himself gesturing around the ship. "Now, chasin' whales ain't all you'll be doin'. We don't spot 'em every day, so there's plenty of work to go around. When you're not out on the boats, you'll be helpin' with the riggin', helping the cook, whatever needs doin' to keep the ship in order. The sea's unforgivin', and the *Herald* needs to be in good shape if we're to survive it."

Silas took the harpoon from Doyle, his expression softening slightly. "Look, I know it sounds like a lot, but you'll get the hang of it. Every man's got his first time out at sea, and the captain wouldn't have picked you for this job if he didn't think you could handle it."

Doyle felt the pressure of his new role, but Silas' confidence was reassuring.

"One more thing," Silas added, grinning. "When the time comes, don't be thinkin' too much. Just trust your gut, let her fly, and the lads will do the rest."

Chapter
Into the Frozen Unknown

The cold was a living thing in the Arctic, seeping into bones, stealing breath, and gnawing at exposed skin. As the *Herald* pushed its way through the unforgiving ice flows, its timbers groaned under the weight of the frozen wind. All around stretched a vast, desolate expanse of blue and white, broken only by towering icebergs that loomed like silent sentinels over the frozen sea.

Forced to sail in these inhospitable waters was a small revenge for the majestic sea mammals under deadly pursuit. Whales, like salmon, traveled to the waters of their birth to spawn. As a result, whaling ships were obliged to follow whales to their breeding grounds in the inhospitable Arctic. There, they hoped to make their fortune by filling the insatiable needs of society. Whale oil provided illumination in oil lamps and lubrication for industrial machinery along with acting as a key ingredient in everything from women's cosmetics to food.

Doyle found himself satisfying the needs of his personal economic need by standing on the frozen deck, pulling his heavy woolen coat that much tighter. His breath clouded in the freezing air as his gloved hands trembled.

"Ye look frozen already, lad," came the voice of Captain Garret, gruff and seasoned. "Still, fer a young lad, it's got all the makings of a grand adventure, don't it?"

Doyle managed a smile through his chattering teeth. "Aye, Captain. It's certainly unlike anything I've ever experienced before."

Garret chuckled, a sound rough as the wind. "Nothin' like the streets o' Scotland, eh? This here's the wild frontier—nothin' but ice an' death if ye ain't careful."

The captain's words struck Doyle more deeply than he'd expected. "I've seen dead men," Doyle replied, trying to sound confident, though it came out more defensive than a boast. "But seeing somebody die is another thing."

Garret nodded, his eyes narrowing as he scanned the horizon. "Aye, it's a whole different beast. This be the kind o' place that'll test a man's spirit—break 'im clean if he ain't strong enough. Seen plenty o' sailors lose their nerve out here."

Doyle fell silent, the weight of the journey ahead settling in. He had been drawn to this voyage for what he perceived as easy money. But now, surrounded by the vast, unforgiving ice, he realized just how foolish that thought had been.

"I'll make it, Captain," Doyle said, his voice steadier this time.

Garret clapped a hand on his shoulder, offering a rare smile. "Silas tells me ye've got the makin's of a first-rate harpooner."

Before Doyle could say a word, a lookout's voice cut through the cold air.

"Ship ahead!"

Garret's face hardened, his eyes narrowed toward the horizon where the outline of a vessel could just be seen through the mist and ice. Doyle squinted, barely making out the ghostly silhouette of what looked like a ship swallowed by ice flows.

"I'll bring us closer," Garret said, his tone suddenly serious. "Could be survivors—or worse."

Chapter
The Derelict

The *Herald* groaned as it slowed its approach, floating ice bouncing off the hull. All eyes were on the ghostly silhouette that emerged from the mist—a ship, its once-proud sails now little more than tattered rags fluttering in the frigid air. The vessel loomed eerily before them, an unnatural stillness surrounding it, as though it were frozen in time along with the unforgiving ice.

Doyle stood at the bow, his pulse quickening as they drew closer. The ship looked ancient, worn by the elements, its hull damaged by ice and snow. The name, *Octavius,* became visible.

"It can't be," said Captain Garret in an uncharacteristically shaken voice.

"Why can't it be, skipper?" asked Doyle.

Garret grasped the rail to steady himself. "There's a sea tale 'bout the *Octavius*. They say her crew, in their folly, tried cuttin' their journey short from the Orient back to England by takin' the Northwest Passage. She vanished more'n ten years ago."

"I don't understand," observed a confused Doyle."I've always understood that nobody's ever found the passage because it's usually frozen over, or changes with the ice flows. All ships take the longer route around Cape Horn."

"Aye, that's it exactly," said Garret. "They've been chasin' that bloody passage fer centuries—men like Franklin, Parry, an' Hudson. Most of 'em, fine explorers they were, vanished without a trace and froze solid. Thinkin' they could find a shortcut to the Orient through the ice—it's a fool's errand, lad. Too many ships an' too many lives lost to the false hope o' riches buried beyond the cold."

"So, why would a merchant ship attempt it when professional explorers failed?"

"I dunno, but they did give it a go. An' looks like they made it, 'cause here she is—if it's the same ship..." Garret turned to the assembled crew. "We'll keep our distance. Get the whaleboat ready to see what's what, and keep yer wits sharp."

Soon, a boat was launched with MacLeod, Winthrop, Moore, Captain Garret, Doyle and Li, the cook. Each had a designated area to check.

There was still no movement on the derelict's deck. As they rowed closer, the heavy silence grew more oppressive.

"Captain," Doyle finally ventured, his breath fogging in the cold as their boat approached the hull." Do you think people could still be aboard?"

Garret turned, his expression grim. "If there are, lad, they'll be frozen solid by now. No man survives long in this cold."

After MacLeod made two attempts to hail the crew, they tied-up alongside the *Octavius*. The only sound was the creaking of frozen timbers, as though the ship itself was groaning under the weight of its past. The boat crew hesitated, eyes wide as they stared at the frozen wreck.

"Let's move, men," Garret ordered, snapping them out of their stupor. "Doyle, you're with me."

Doyle swallowed hard but nodded. They tied-off the whaleboat and clambered over the side. The moment his boots hit the deck, Doyle felt the cold in a new way. It wasn't just the icy wind or the frost that coated every surface. There was something else—a deep, unnatural chill that seeped from the very wood beneath his feet. The deck was eerily quiet, the lines stiff with ice and the rigging hanging limp as though the ship had been abandoned for decades. No signs of life. No movement. Nothing.

Garret motioned for the men to go to the areas they were designated to search. "Watch yourselves."

Doyle followed closely behind Garret as they moved toward the aft quarters. Each step felt heavy, the wood beneath them creaking in protest as though warning them to turn back.

The berths at the stern were as frozen as the rest of the ship. A thin layer of frost covered the walls, and the smell of wood decay hung faintly in the air. The captain's cabin was small, with a desk and a few scattered charts. But what caught Doyle's eye was the figure slumped over the desk. His body, long dead, was frozen in place, still gripping a quill as though he'd been writing when the cold overtook him. His face, half-covered in ice, was contorted in an expression of fear with eyes wide and empty.

Garret leaned forward, his breath shallow. "The captain, I reckon."

Doyle nodded, his stomach twisting at the sight. He had seen corpses before, but not like this. The man looked as though he had been trying to outrun the grim reaper. On the desk lay a logbook, the pages brittle with age and cold. Doyle reached for it, carefully prying the frozen pages apart. The last entry was dated over a dozen years back—1866. The last words were scrawled weakly:

"We're trapped with no way out. At least the voices will soon stop. I can hear them, whispering in the wind."

Doyle closed the book and put it in his medical bag. Garret had gone pale beneath his weathered skin. Neither of them spoke, but the weight of the discovery hung heavy between them. Midshipman Winthrop appeared in the doorway and broke the silence. "Captain, there's more bodies forward."

Next to the master's cabin they found a frozen woman and child in a bunk. The woman was clutching the boy of about 5 years of age.   She appeared to be Asian while the boy was half caucasian.

"The skipper's family I presume," said Garret.

"At least they died together," said Doyle making a cursory examination. "There are no signs of injuries. However, it appears that they're malnourished."

"Poor buggers probably got caught in the ice and ran out of food. We'll know for sure when Li checks the pantry. It's how the ship made it this far that's the real mystery?"

"How's that, Captain?"

"Here in the Arctic, a ship's only chance of survivin' the winter's to find a safe spot to anchor—somewhere sheltered behind a bit o' land. Ye need a place where the ice can't pile up and crush the hull—where the floes won't press in. Like hidin' behind a rock when the storm's blowin' fierce. Without it, the ice moves and shifts, squeezin' the ship till she cracks and splinters. There's no mercy in that ice. But the *Octavius* was adrift fer twelve years without a live soul aboard to guide her to the next safe harbor come spring. How the devil could she make it through twelve seasons without bein' crushed? No hands to steer, no crew to keep her safe from the ice. It ain't possible... unless somethin' else was watchin' over her—somethin' beyond what we can reckon."

After more examination, they moved forward toward the bow and found more frozen crew - mostly in their bunks. A cursory examination of each yielded the same results. However, two men wrapped in canvas had a different story to tell.

"Look at this, skipper," said Doyle. "There are rope burns on his neck. Feeling along the spine I can tell that his neck's been clean broken."

"So you think he was hung?" before awaiting an answer, Garret poked his head into the passage leading to deck and yelled, "MacLeod, check the yard arms to see if there's anything amiss."

"Yes, he was hanged," continued Doyle. "This other man has a contusion in his skull. Looks like he died from that injury."

"Could it have been a fall?"

"I don't think so," said Doyle looking closer. "See how its only a half inch wide. I'd wager a marlin spike."

A marlin spike was a tapered metal rod common to most sailors. The tool was pointed at one end and blunt at the other to loosen stubborn knots in lines.

"So he was done in," said Garret.

MacLeod then appeared and made his report. "There's a line on one of the yardarms. Looks to have been a noose." MacLeod then looked at the other body Doyle was examining and saw the hole in his head. "Pardon me skipper, but this ship is cursed. We need to muster up the lads and get out of here."

"I need more time, captain," objected Doyle. "We don't know what caused all this."

Captain Garret thought form a moment, then responded. " Sorry, Doyle. I've seen some queer things in my years at sea, but nothin' beats this. We'll learn what we can from Li 'bout the food stores, and Moore 'bout the cargo, while Mr. MacLeod makes to push off. The boarding party'll meet up later on the *Herald* to piece it all together."

Doyle was about to object again, but thought better of it. Garret expected his orders to be followed without question. They arrived at the pantry and found Li gone.

"Let's get to the whaleboat and collect Li along the way," ordered Garret.

Glancing at MacLoud, Garret remarked in a low voice… "The boys are rightly spooked. I'll have a mutiny if I keep them here much longer."

The ship appeared to groan as if confirming Garret's fears. Even Doyle was ready to leave. Whatever had happened on the *Octavius*, it seemed that the ghostly crew weren't at rest. As they clambered toward the whaleboat, Winthrop reported that Li and Moore were still unaccounted for.

"Hell's teeth, I'll fetch them myself," growled Garret.

After what seemed an eternity, Garret, Li and Moore appeared on deck.

"What did you find, Mr. Li?" asked Doyle.

"No food in pantry. I go below to help Mr. Moore, but he hear me come and shout he already finish."

"Let's keep our minds on gettin' back to the *Herald* and sortin' out what's happened where it's safe, aboard our own ship," said Garret gesturing toward the whaleboat.

The journey back to the *Herald* was silent as the grave. It was as if each man was in shock from the experience and wanted to pretend it didn't happen.

Chapter
The Debate

On arrival at the *Herald*, they filed in the Galley. Each man found a spot at a table and waited for Garret to speak.

Garret turned to Moore and said,"What was in the hold?"

"Normal cases, barrels and bags with a Chinese marking, skipper. I broke open a bag or two and found grain and dried leaves."

Li interjected, "Marking looked Chinese, but not. Make no sense to me."

"You said they were last in the Orient, skipper," observed Doyle. "Are the contents typical of the spice trade?"

"I suppose so," responded Garret. "It sounds like spices and tea."

"Can we return tomorrow and grab a sample of each? They might have a bearing on what happened... " asked Doyle as he retrieved the ships log from his medical bag and placed it on the table.

Before Garret could answer, MacLeod interjected while staring at Doyle. "It ain't right you taking that book."

Doyle was taken aback and responded sarcastically. "If it's one thing I've learned in medical school. It's that the dead don't talk. So, we need the book to determine what happened - nothing can hurt us now."

The other men chuckled uneasily, but MacLeod didn't smile. Instead, he cleared his throat, his deep voice filling the cold air like the rumble of distant thunder.

"I've seen things, Doyle," his eyes narrowing. "Out here on the water, the world operates on a different set of rules. If those rules are broken, no living thing can save you. One of those rules is that you don't take the property of a dead sailor. If you do, the sea will take its revenge."

Doyle tried to look disinterested and stared down at the book while the rest of the crew shuffled slightly in their seats. MacLeod's stories were always dark and generally tinged with the supernatural, but this one seemed different—more personal, more real.

Garret sighed at the interruption, but gave MacLeod a nod. "Go on, lad, tell Doyle yer story… he's gotta learn…"

"It was years ago," MacLeod continued, his voice low, "on a whaler called the *Resolute*, out in the Arctic, east of Baffin Bay. The ice had closed in tight around us, just like it did here. We were stuck for days—weeks maybe. The cold does strange things to a man when he's trapped like that. One day, we lost a sailor. His name was Jim Macready—a strong lad, too proud for his own good. He went out on the ice to check the lines on a boat tied to the side of the ship. Must've slipped, they said, and fell into the freezing water below. By the time they hauled him back up, he was dead. Frozen solid, like a statue of ice."

The men around the tables shifted uncomfortably. They had all seen men lost to the sea, but this story was beginning to take a darker turn. They could visualize in their mind's eye the *Octavius* rising and falling in the waves nearby as if confirming MacLoud's words.

"Now, Macready had a few prized possessions—things he kept close," MacLeod went on, his eyes gleaming with the memory. "A silver locket, some old coins, and a leather-bound book he always carried, though he never let anyone see what was inside. When we pulled him out of the water, the captain decided to bury him in the ice—no time to return home, no way to do it proper."

MacLeod paused, leaning forward and continued. "But a few of the men—well, they didn't think Macready's things should go down with him. The locket, the coins, the book—they took them, each man keeping something for himself. I warned them, told 'em it wasn't right, but they wouldn't listen."

The room seemed to grow even colder, as if a ghost entered the room. Doyle felt a shiver crawl up his spine, though he said nothing. "Soon after that," MacLeod said, his voice taking on a darker edge, "things started happening. Small things at first. One man, Harwell, swore he heard footsteps on the deck one night, even though no one else was around. Another, Callahan, woke up in the middle of the night with his blanket soaking wet, like he'd been dragged into the sea. None of them thought much of it—just the cold playing tricks. But then one of them—Callahan—went mad. Said he saw Macready standing at the foot of his bunk, dripping with ice water, his dead eyes staring right at him. Callahan started screaming, wouldn't stop until they tied him down."

MacLeod's deep-set eyes reflected off the porthole light. "The next night, they found Callahan dead—face down in a puddle of water in his bunk. His mouth was open, as if he'd been trying to scream, but no sound had come out."

Doyle said nothing, the tension was palpable.

"They found Macready's book under Callahan's pillow," MacLeod said, his voice barely a whisper now. "The same one he'd stolen off Macready's body. But the book was frozen solid—ice covered every page."

Doyle had heard enough and purposely closed the book with a clap.

"Well the pages of *this* book work just fine and are completely legible. So, I believe the captain and crew are still on the *Octavius*," replied Doyle.

The other crewman responded with nervous chuckles.

"Laugh if you want," retorted MacLeod. "But Harwell and the rest - they never made it back. We left the ice, but each man who took something from Macready was dead before we reached port. Drowned, frozen, or worse. You don't take from the dead, Doyle. Not without paying the price. The sea... it remembers."

Captain Garret had listened patiently, but decided to draw the gathering to a conclusion. "The *Octavius* crew did the unthinkable—they made it through the Northwest Passage. For that, they deserve to be remembered as the first. So, Doyle'll transcribe their last log entries, and we'll hand it over to the admiralty with our affidavits as proof o' their feat. Two of us'll take the log back to the *Octavius* tomorrow, set her up for a tow, and get her to a safe anchorage at Baffin Island. That'll keep her from bein' crushed by the sea ice till the admiralty can deal with her proper."

"I'll go with you to set-up the tow, captain" offered Doyle. "I'll finish my ..."

"That won't be needed," said Garret. "I ain't riskin' the crew more'n I have to. I'll coxswain the whaleboat meself to set the bowline, and Moore'll see to it everythin', includin' the cargo, is secure for sea. Once it's done, we'll drop the *Octavius*' anchor at Baffin Island an' be off quick as a wink."

"And never look back," interjected MacLoud.

Chapter
Ship's Log

Doyle retreated to his quarters in sickbay where he went to a small writing table and retrieved paper and pen from a small desk table. He then began to transcribe the derelict's last events from the log as Garret had ordered.

Octavius
(Captain's entries during the weeks preceding the final entry)

September 12, 1868
We've changed course, heading for the Northwest Passage. The decision to take this route weighs heavy, but no one questions me outright - only I know the drive of Thistle Mountain. There's something wrong with the wind, and the ice seems to thicken faster than it should. Winter's coming early. We're too far northeast of Point Barrow now to turn back.

September 18, 1868
The ice is thickening day by day. We push forward, but each hour it grows more treacherous. I fear we'll be trapped if we don't find a way through soon. Some of the crew are showing signs of wear, but it's more than just the cold. A tension hangs in the air. I wonder if the cargo we took on in the Orient is at fault.

September 24, 1868

Paranoia spreads like ice around us. Men whisper of seeing things in the fog—shapes that vanish when looked at directly. The nights are colder, longer, and the winds howl like the voices of the dead. Halliday swears he saw something moving between the ice floes. I keep a brave face, but there's a deep sense of foreboding.

September 29, 1868

We're surrounded by pack ice now, and the crew grows restless. Jenkins told me of a dream where the ship was crushed by ice, its timbers splintering like bones. Others speak of nightmares—shadows on the deck, voices calling their names from the darkness. I fear the cold is warping their minds. Winter is coming fast, too fast.

October 3, 1868

Simmons killed Jenkins today. He said Jenkins was a demon, disguised as a man. The men are rattled, the ice cracking and groaning around us, like a cage closing in. We put Simmons on trial before the mast and passed sentence of a dozen lashes. I wonder if something followed us from the East, something we shouldn't have brought aboard. The crew's fear grows, and I can do little to ease it.

October 8, 1868

The ice is now completely impenetrable. We've lost all hope of returning. Men undeniably see figures in the mist— specters moving silently across the ice. Rations are low, and so is our sanity. I regret the decision to take on that strange cargo in Canton. We should've stayed clear of the Orient.

October 13, 1868

Another crewman lost—Davies. We found him hanging from the mainmast. The cold is too much for most now. Food is scarce, but even those who can eat refuse. Some claim the ship is cursed, that something in the hold is poisoning us. I fear they might be right.

October 15, 1868

We are surrounded by unyielding ice. The cold bites deep, but worse still are the hallucinations. Last night, I saw my wife and son in the fog, standing on the ice, staring at me. I tore away from the vision to find them in bed. The others report similar visions. They barely move now, huddling together, whispering of ghosts. I doubt we'll survive much longer.

October 18, 1868

Starvation has claimed us, but the real killer is something else. There's no way out now. It will be a disappointment to My King.

We're trapped with no way out. At least the voices will soon stop. I can hear them, whispering in the wind.

47

Little did Doyle know that *Heralds'* log would soon mirror the *Octavius* as they fought for their own survival.

Chapter
Octavius Put to Rest

As the whaleboat left the derelict ship, Doyle could see Captain Garret and Moore rowing with a steady rhythm, their faces set with a grim determination. The *Octavius* now lay anchored in the cove behind them, silhouetted against the rising cliffs of Baffin Island. Doyle watched the whaleboat drawing closer. To his surprise, both men had rifles slung across their shoulders, glinting in the pale Arctic light.

"I don't recall you bringing weapons when you left, Captain," Doyle remarked when they returned and secured the boat on its davits.

"Aye, Mr. Doyle," Garret said patting the stock of his rifle. "Ghosts or no ghosts, I felt safer takin' a rifle aboard that cursed ship."

Moore nodded in agreement, his knuckles still white as he gripped the gun. "Even if they be dead, I'd rather face 'em armed."

Doyle nodded thoughtfully, noting the stressed faces of both men. There was no need to ask if they had found anything unusual on the *Octavius*. Their silence, combined with the uneasy way they held their weapons, was answer enough.

As the *Herald* got underway, a bitter wind cut through the coats and scarves of the crew gathered on deck. All eyes were fixed on the haunting sight of the *Octavius* sitting eerily still in a forbidding land. The anchorage itself was isolated, concealed from any wandering eye, as though nature itself sought to bury the *Octavius* in its frozen grasp. The unforgiving cold would soon entomb the derelict into place with immovable ice. She would lay there as a forgotten relic, untouched and unseen, her secrets trapped with her in the depths of the far North. Doyle gripped the railing, unable to shake the feeling that they had witnessed something from another world.

"No sailers will bother her there," muttered MacLoud.

Once they reached a safe distance, Doyle satisfied his curiosity and questioned Garret. "Did you learn anything more when you returned the log and rigged for towing?"

"Aye, nuthin', Mr. Doyle. I tossed that blasted log back where we found it in that cursed cabin and bolted straight for the deck. Mr. Moore and me stayed topside till we was safe back aboard the *Herald*. No sense in wakin' the dead."

Moore, standing nearby, nodded his confirmation, "When I went below to secure the cargo, I saw that same Chinese marking."

"Did you check the contents of any more barrels and crates?"

"Like the skipper said...no sense in staying longer than I had to. I hotfooted it topside."

Maybe it was just as well. If ever there was a place to leave bad memories *and* the dead, it was Baffin Island.

England 1900
(the present)

"I suppose not," agreed Doyle. "And to my knowledge, the captain never said another word. He knew it would be the end of all our careers. The captain said he never mentioned in the report any details like our examination of the *Octavius* bodies or the cargo. He only admitted to retrieving the log to get them credit. He never said anything about *you know who's* death."

"I read newspapers afterward - saw nothing. So, I think report died in Navy, government," said Li.

"I agree," said Baines."The admiralty probably buried it in the archives not wanting to create a ghost story. Did anybody meet this Madame Seraphine somewhere - at the theater perhaps?"

"Only I and Doyle frequent the theater where she hails and I never made her acquaintance," said Winthrop. "That only leaves you Doyle…"

Doyle frowned, his brows knitting together. "Not I. I've tried to find out where she came from and can't find a trace."

"So, she just appeared like a shadow drifting into the harbor with all the rest of the fog," mused Moore. "Maybe she really was hailed from a world beyond the grave. She seems to be a bonafide medium."

"I'm not convinced of that," countered Doyle. "Lets just assume she heard some rumor of the *Octavius* through an admiralty archivist. Then she researched the *Herald* and found its whereabouts and the rest of us."

"But why would she care?" asked Baines with a whine.

"To further her show, I'll wager," said Winthrop.

"Either way," observed Doyle. "We'll find out tonight."

Chapter
The Seance

The *Herald*'s galley, usually a place of warmth and rough camaraderie, now felt like a tomb. The low flicker of a single candle cast long shadows that danced upon the aged wood, barely keeping encroaching darkness at bay. The air was heavy, almost stifling, as if the ship itself held its breath, waiting for what was to come.

Madame Seraphine sat at the table, her hands outstretched with fingertips barely brushing the cold surface. The crew, Doyle among them, sat in a rough circle, eyes shifting between one another with nervous anticipation. Seraphine's face was pale, her usual theatrical grace giving way to something more solemn. The galley seemed to creak and groan in time with her low, steady voice as she began the seance.

"We gather here, not just as people of the living, but to reach beyond the veil of death," Seraphine intoned, her voice barely more than a whisper. "Those who seek answers, those who wander still... we call to you. Show yourselves."

The lamp seemed to dim, its light faltering as the ship groaned again, more insistently this time, as though the very planks beneath their feet were stirring. The coldness that had begun to creep in from the outside suddenly intensified, sending a chill. Doyle felt the hairs on the back of his neck prickle as a strange noise, faint at first, began to emerge from the recesses of the ship. A distant creaking, like a door swinging slowly on rusted hinges.

Seraphine's voice deepened as she spoke. "Captain of the *Octavius*, you who sought to sail through the frozen seas, reveal yourself. We summon you now. Come to us."

The air grew thicker, the unmistakable sound of boots echoed, slow and deliberate. Doyle's heart raced as the candle flickered once more, the flame sputtering as if fighting to stay alive. And then, from the shadows, a figure began to materialize — tall, gaunt, dressed in the tattered remains of a mariner's coat and captain's hat. His eyes were hollow, his face as pale as the Arctic ice itself.

The figure channeled his raspy voice through Seraphine. "Why did I steer my ship into those cursed waters?"

His eyes seemed to scan the room through unseeing eyes for something lost. His voice, through Seraphine, trembled with regret. "I... I was deceived by promises of shortcuts. But the cold... the ice is unforgiving."

Something rattled the table, as though the captain's words summoned the frozen winds of the Arctic into the room. The crew shifted uncomfortably, some muttering prayers under their breath.

Seraphine spoke again, her own voice coaxing. "Who deceived you, Captain, who sent you to your doom?"

The captain's form wavered, his face contorted in agony. "We should never have taken it... cursed. Cursed us all."

With that, the captain's image faded into the shadows, leaving the room in silence save for the sound of shallow breathing from the crew.

Doyle had barely time to collect his thoughts when a soft, childish laugh cut through the air from Seraphine's mouth. The galley grew colder still. From beneath the table, small footsteps pattered on the floorboards, like the sound of bare feet on wood. Madame Seraphine's eyes closed as her voice softened.

"Child of the lost, we welcome you. Come to us."

The candle sputtered again before revealing the small figure of a child, no more than six years old. He stood, half hidden in shadow, clutching a tattered doll. His eyes, wide and unblinking, stared up at Seraphine. Doyle's breath caught in his throat.

"Mama?" the child whispered, his voice channeled through Seraphine was high and soft, yet clear enough to send a shiver down every spine in the room. "Mama, where are you?"

Another figure emerged—this one taller, cloaked in dark rags. The mother, her face lined with sorrow, stood by the child. She hovered with a sluggish grace, her fingers extended as if trying to hold onto something she could no longer grasp. "We should not have come," the mother's channeled voice said, her voice full of regret. "We should have thought better."

Doyle swallowed hard, his heart pounding as the mother and child's forms began to fade. Seraphine's hands trembled, her face drawn tight with concentration as she continued.

"We summon one more. The man who took his own life. Show yourself."

Cold air seemed to extinguish one of the lamps. From the darkness, a figure stepped forward, its form hunched, a rope still hanging loosely around its neck. The crewman who had ended his own life. His face was gaunt, his eyes wide with terror, as though he still saw whatever had driven him to despair.

"I saw things that cannot be and voices that deceived. Now I'm no more," said the channeled voice.

His form flickered like a candle in the wind before vanishing completely. The room was plunged into silence once more.

Doyle, heart still pounding, cast a glance toward Madame Seraphine. She sat motionless, eyes closed, her breathing heavy, as if the weight of summoning the dead and channeling their voices had drained her. He resolved to pull himself together and begin his investigation. His fingers traced the underside of the table, where they brushed against something that caught his attention—a faint protrusion, smooth yet slightly out of place on the worn wood. It could have been nothing, just a quirk of the old ship. He made a mental note to inspect it after the seance.

"We are not finished," Seraphine said, her voice hollow. "There is another soul, one of the *Herald*. He calls out…"

From the far corner of the galley, where the shadows seemed to pool like dark water, a figure began to take shape. At first, it was nothing more than a wavering silhouette, but as it solidified, the crew around the table gasped in unison.

Standing before them, clad in the stained, worn garb of a whaler, was Silas Lentz, the *Herald*'s harpooner lost during the troubles. His figure was strikingly vivid, his muscular arms hanging limp by his sides, his once-tanned face now pale and translucent. A deep scar shown on his head, the mark of a violent end. His eyes, dark and penetrating, seemed to hover over the room. The air felt electric, charged with a tension that made Doyle's skin prickle. He had seen Silas in life, and this apparition was absolutely accurate, down to the harpoon tattoo inked on the sailor's forearm. This didn't look like a vague spirit, it was Silas.

Whispers rippled through the room as the men shifted uncomfortably in their seats. No one had expected this, least of all Doyle, who was gripping the edge of the table with white-knuckled intensity.

Silas' voice, when he finally spoke through Seraphine, was a low rasp, as if his throat still bore the scars of his final moments.

"I stand here... because my death was no accident. I was murdered."

A collective intake of breath filled the galley. The word "murdered" hung in the air like a curse, seeping into the minds of the men seated around the table. Doyle could see the tension rising, the flickers of fear in the crew's eyes. Someone shifted uncomfortably and another muttered a quick prayer under his breath. Silas' gaze hovered intently on the room once more.

"The guilty... in this room..."

The participants recoiled, some visibly shaking, their hands gripping the edge of the table like a lifeline. Doyle's mind raced, every instinct telling him to stay silent, to let the seance unfold naturally. But he couldn't stop himself. The tension was unbearable.

"Silas," Doyle called out, his voice sharper than intended. "We tried to figure it out, you must know that. We couldn't discern man nor spirit during the chaos. Who killed you? Tell us."

Silas' form flickered slightly and the edges of his figure began blurring as though dissolving into mist. "I will return..."

Before Doyle could speak again, the figure dissipated into the surrounding shadows, leaving only the faintest trace of his presence — a coldness that lingered in the air, a silence that seemed to press down on all. The gas lamps on the walls were lit casting the room into stark brightness once more. The seance was over, but the room remained tense. Madame Seraphine slumped forward, her breathing heavy and labored, as if pulling back from the edge of death itself had drained her completely.

Chapter
Crew Reflections

When the seance concluded, captain and crew alike bolted for the deck, nearly tripping over each other in their rush to escape. The air had grown thick with dread, and even the seasoned sailors seemed rattled by what they'd just witnessed. Doyle remained behind, casting a glance toward Madame Seraphine who sat at the table weeping quietly. Her sobs were barely audible, but the sight of her trembling shoulders spoke louder than words.

"Why are you crying?" Doyle asked gently. "Most mediums I've observed only act exhausted after such displays. What affected you so deeply?"

Seraphine hesitated, wiping at her eyes with trembling hands. "It was the child," she whispered after a long pause. "Seeing him... it was more than I expected. It—" She faltered, as if searching for the right words. "It touched something deep within me."

Doyle watched her, suspicion gnawing at him, but he held his tongue. Without another word, he turned and headed for the deck. As he emerged into the brisk night air, he found the crew in an animated discussion, their voices raised in nervous excitement.

"She must be the real thing," MacLeod insisted, his eyes wide. "Silas was there! The spitting image of him, I swear it. None of us ever told anyone 'bout how he died... those strange circumstances."

Doyle joined them and they immediately turned his way, questioning eyes full of uncertainty.

"How in God's name could Silas be so real?" Moore asked, his voice trembling. "We all saw him, didn't we? The way he stood there, lookin' just like he did before he... before he died. How could she have known? No one told her a thing about Silas, not the way he went."

Winthrop nodded fervently. "It was him, I swear it. The face, the way he spoke. No one else could've known that... not even her."

They turned to Doyle, desperate for answers. "Is she real, Doyle? Was that truly Silas?"

Doyle sighed, rubbing the back of his neck. "I don't know," he admitted, feeling the weight of their collective stares. "I agree, it was the spitting image of Silas. Maybe she does have some gift, but I've seen fakes do things that seem just as impossible with tricks and gadgets. I need more time to investigate - I've been deceived before."

MacLeod made his way to the gangplank, "I ain't waiting around for no investigation by a magazine detective - especially one outwitted by little girls."

Doyle reacted to the obvious reference to the Cottingley Fairies debacle.

Before MacLeod could start down the gangplank, Captain Garrett stepped forward and blocked his path. His weathered face was stern, voice firm with authority, "That's enough. Nobody leaves this ship. Doing so is as good as confessin' to killing Silas. Plus, you won't receive your £100 till the *Herald* goes for scrap. You can figure something out by then, can't you, Doyle?"

Doyle pondered the question. "I don't know. But I can do my best to finish in a few days, maybe a week."

The men started to object.

"If Doyle can't solve this in a week, you can go on your merry way and get your £100," said Garret pacifying to group.

After some rumbling, everyone resigned themselves to the situation. One by one, they proceeded to their own berth to brood in silence, suspicion hanging in the air like a specter.

Chapter
The Galley

Doyle made his way back to the galley hoping to talk to Madame Seraphine. When he arrived, the room was empty. He noticed a folded note left neatly on the table addressed to him. He picked it up and read the brief message: *"This is much harder than I expected, but I will be back to see it through... trust me."*

Doyle puzzled at the note that seemed sincere and almost vulnerable, totally uncharacteristic for any medium he'd previously encountered. It also seemed to suppose them as intimate friends of sorts. That made no sense given they'd just met. After another read, he tucked the note in his pocket.

He crouched down by the table where he thought he'd detected something earlier and found nothing. He expanded his examination and ran his fingers along the entire underside searching for any hidden mechanisms. He had studied the tricks used by famous frauds like Anna Eva Fay and knew to search for spring-loaded devices that created 'spirit touches' and even breezes. These spiritualists used other techniques including invisible wires and mechanical devices to move objects to simulate supernatural activity. But Doyle found nothing—no wires, no springs. Just smooth wood. If something had been under there earlier, Seraphine or someone else, had removed it.

Next, Doyle's attention was drawn to a thin layer of soot on the floor. He knelt down, examining it more closely. It reminded him of another infamous fraudster, Mina "Margery" Crandon, who used phosphorus powder and other chemical concoctions to create ghostly effects. The soot on the floor could have been from a similar substance. Then again, it might be from the gas lamps in the space.

Doyle stood in silence while his mind buzzed with questions about Seraphine, the seance, and the unnerving appearance of Silas. It *must* be a total fabrication, but it seemed so real. He reminded himself that he had been convinced that the Cottingley Fairies seemed genuine, even to the photographic expert he'd hired thought so.

Doyle reached into his pocket, feeling the folded note again. *"This is much harder than I expected, but I will be back to see it through...trust me."*

Her words, though cryptic, weighed heavily. Doyle's instincts told him that whatever was happening here was more than just a seance. His thoughts went back to the event itself, to the moment when Silas appeared. It had been so convincing — the look of him, the tone of his voice channeled through Seraphine. The resemblance had been too perfect. Doyle sighed, and rubbed his temples. It was so easy to create stories with clues contrived to display a detective's brilliance. This was something else entirely.

Seraphine breaking character at the end of the seance nagged at him. She had been genuinely upset, crying quietly when everyone else had rushed to the deck. Most mediums he'd seen only feigned exhaustion or claimed spiritual after-effects. When he asked why she was so shaken, her answer had been vague — the child's spirit had affected her deeply. *But was that the truth, or was it something else entirely?*

The note suggested she was struggling with something. Perhaps it was the weight of her own deception or maybe a deeper connection to the spirits she claimed to summon. He tried to remove her image from his mind. He was too mesmerized by the striking woman and couldn't think straight.

Doyle returned his focus again to the room. Every physical trace of the seance had been carefully erased. Exasperated, Doyle made his way to the door. He needed to think and trudged back to his quarters in sick bay. There his mind returned to Silas and the Arctic long ago.

70

Arctic 1878
(20 years earlier)

Chapter
Sick Call

A full day had passed since leaving the *Octavius* and stars began to prick the inky sky. Luckily, sailors had a time honored nightly routine to keep them from focusing on the prior days events - starting with a change of the watch. Men shuffled onto deck, their boots scuffing against the worn wooden planks, while those who had finished their shift gratefully descended below, seeking rest in the cramped quarters. The ship's lanterns were lit, their dim, flickering glow casting long, wavering shadows across the deck and rigging.

Sailors not on watch would carve scrimshaw on whale bones or pass a few quiet words with a crew mate. Tonight, however, each man kept to himself. The captain maintained a vigil occasionally pacing the deck.

Doyle listened through the porthole of his sickbay quarters for any unusual activity. He heard Garret give an instruction to the watch stander nearest him. Otherwise, everyone was quiet as the grave. Doyle found himself in much the same state while trying to focus on a book.

A smiling Silas appeared at the doorway, his silhouette framed by the lantern's soft glow.

"Silas! Come in," Doyle said warmly, waving him over. "I'm glad for a visitor after this nasty business. What brings you here?"

Silas stepped into the room, but something about his posture was off. Normally steady and confident, the young harpooner seemed hesitant. His usually bright eyes appeared dimmed, and he blinked more often than usual, as if trying to clear his vision.

Doyle's smile faded. "You alright? You look... off."

Silas sat down heavily on a nearby bench, rubbing his temples. "That's what I came to talk to you about," he muttered. "Something's... not right with me."

Alarmed, Doyle leaned forward. "What do you mean?"

Silas shifted uncomfortably, glancing around the room as if unsure how to explain the strange symptoms. "It's hard to say, exactly. Yesterday I got confused in the weapons locker with the guns. Captain Garret met me and set things straight as best he could. This morning I woke up and my vision was strange, affecting my balance. I seem to have lost my sea legs. The lamps..." He trailed off, staring at the lantern hanging from the ceiling. "The lamps, they're movin'—more than they should. Like... more than the ship's rollin'."

Doyle raised an eyebrow, his concern deepening. "You're seeing things?"

Silas nodded, his expression tense. "Aye, but just little things, like the lamps flickerin' or movin' wrong. Thought maybe I was just tired, but it ain't goin' away."

Doyle scratched his chin, perplexed. "Anything like this ever happened before?"

Silas shook his head. "Nah. Never. But there's somethin' else. It's like I can't get a solid grip on my surroundings. It's like things are moving in the shadows."

Doyle studied his friend carefully. Silas had been a steady, reliable presence aboard the *Herald*—strong, capable, and more experienced than most men his age. It was unlike him to be rattled.

74

Doyle knew from their time together training together with harpoons that Silas wasn't prone to exaggeration.

"It can't be from the *Octavius,* you stayed on the *Herald* with the rest of the crew. Are you feeling dizzy too…are you in danger of falling if we're called to chase a whale?"

"Not dizziness exactly, but everything feels... out of kilter," Silas said slowly. "Like the ship's rockin' too hard, even when it's barely moving. I've no headaches, but my eyes, they just don't feel right. Can't explain it. I'm not sure I'd be my best in a whale chase."

"Let's take a look," said Doyle reaching for a magnifying glass. He examined his eyes noting that they were slightly dilated. He took his pulse and found it modestly quickened - but nothing too extreme. His heart and lungs sounded normal. "You're basically in good shape. Could be something you ate, or maybe it's fatigue catching up with you…"

Silas didn't seem convinced. He gave a half-hearted chuckle. "You're thinkin' some bad food from our less than honest supply officer is responsible for my sea legs goin' after all these years?"

"Maybe," Doyle said, forcing a smile. "But I'll keep an eye on you. I don't think you're in actual danger. Let's not jump to conclusions just yet. I'll place you on sick call - so no night watch. I can give you a sedative to sleep if you'd like…"

"No," said Silas. "I'm tired and will probably fall asleep when I hit the bunk."

Doyle reached out and placed a reassuring hand on his friend's shoulder. Silas nodded, though his usual easy confidence was gone. As he stood to leave, Doyle could see him sway slightly, catching himself against the wall before offering a weak smile. "Thanks, Doc. Just... let me know if you figure somethin' out."

With that, he left the cabin. Doyle couldn't shake the unsettling feeling that this was the beginning of something bad.

Chapter
Moore

The next morning, the low light of the rising sun filtered through the small, salt-encrusted windows of Captain Garrett's cabin, casting a dim glow over the modest space. The room was cluttered but orderly with navigational charts neatly folded on the table, brass instruments polished and glinting faintly in the morning light. A large oak desk sat against the far wall, its surface neatly contained a logbook and a quill pen resting in an ink bottle. The scent of old sea air mingled with the faint traces of tobacco smoke, and the captain's bunk, built into the wall, remained tightly made reflecting Garrett's disciplined nature. Above the desk hung a faded painting of a ship at full sail, its glory slightly dulled with time, much like the captain's hopes for a peaceful voyage.

Doyle sat across from Garrett, the heavy wooden chair creaking under him as the ship gently swayed. Garrett leaned back in his own chair with a look of concern. "You say Silas came to see you and acted strange."

"Yes. He's unsteady and confused. I put him on sick call and sent him to bed."

"When'd it begin?"

"After the weapons locker," said Doyle trying to recall the details of the conversation.

"What 'bout the weapons locker?"

"He didn't say what triggered it. He just said he was confused and then the symptoms began to grow later."

"It's gotta be tied to the whole business with the *Octavius*, Doyle. Ain't no other explanation."

"Silas wasn't on the *Octavius*."

"All the same, there's spiritual things we don't rightly fathom."

"I believe there's some medical explanation. Never-the-less, everyone's spooked and its hard to predict how each man will react."

Garrett grunted. "Aye, they need work to take their minds off it. Idle hands invite trouble. I'll give the crew some extra duties today, keep 'em busy. They can repair the rigging, scrub the decks —anything to keep them from dwelling on... well, on what we've seen."

"I'll give Silas the rest of the day to get get back to normal and interview him again," said Doyle.

After more discussion, Doyle left.

A little while later, the ship's timbers groaned with a commotion topside. Doyle got to his feet and grabbed his coat and made his way up the ladder. The air was thick with shouts and Doyle could already hear Midshipman Winthrop screaming from the cabin he'd just escaped. "Help! Help me! Moore's gone mad in there."

Reaching the door to the deck housing, Doyle tried the handle. It wouldn't budge - locked from the inside.

"Moore!" Garrett bellowed after appearing beside Doyle. "What's happening?"

"Beelzebub... I see you... I see you..." could be heard from inside.

"Moore's got a knife," warned Winthrop.

"Get that hatch open!" Garrett ordered.

Li and Macleod standing nearby heaved their shoulders into the door. Wood groaned and finally gave way with a loud crack. The two men tumbled into the cramped room. Moore stood in the corner, knife in hand, eyes wild, his face twisted with rage. "Beelzebub... You won't get me."

Garret stepped forward, his voice thunderin'. "Put down that blade, Moore. Ain't nothing there!"

For a moment, it was as though Moore didn't hear him. His eyes flickered in the lamplight, scanning the room in a daze. Then, slowly, as if coming out of a dream, his grip loosened, and the knife clattered to the floor. His body sagged, chest heaving with exhaustion, as though whatever possessed him had let go.

Midshipman Winthrop stumbled forward into the room. "He... he kept calling me the devil."

Garrett looked at Moore who crumbled trembling on the floor, muttering incoherently. "What's ailin' him?"

Doyle crouched beside him as he continued to tremble - eyes darting around like a cornered animal. He reached for Moore's wrist, feeling for a pulse. It was fast—but not overly so and there was no sign of fever. Moore kept glancing around wildly, as if trying to focus on something that wasn't there.

Doyle moved Moore's head gently, checking for any signs of injury. The storekeeper had no visible wounds, aside from the sweat beading on his brow and the slight tremor in his hands. His breathing was shallow and erratic, punctuated by muttered words that were nearly incoherent. Doyle leaned closer, trying to make sense of it all.

"Evil eyes... watching..." Moore groaned, his voice cracking.

Doyle glanced up at Garrett. "He's in the throes of some kind of delirium, skipper. We need to calm him down, or he'll harm himself," Then, with steady hands, Doyle retrieved his small medical kit from his pocket. Inside, he found a vial of laudanum containing opium.

"Will that calm him enough?" asked Winthrop, still scared. "We can get restraints…"

"This should sedate him enough for now," Doyle said, carefully measuring a small dose into his syringe—just enough to calm the wild panic without rendering Moore unconscious. Too much could be dangerous, but he had to take the risk. He injected Moore's arm which made him wince slightly, then returned to his wild stare. Doyle watched closely as the laudanum began to take effect. The tremors in Moore's hands slowly subsided, and his breathing evened out. His eyes, though still wide with agitation, seemed to lose some of their frantic edge. The muttering softened, becoming less coherent, as if the man were slipping into a fog.

Garret stood over 'em, arms folded tight. "What could bring this on, Doyle? I've seen men lose their heads to drink or sickness, but this... this feels different. Moore, he *was* with us on the *Octavius*."

Doyle frowned as he stood up, wiping his hands on a rag. "It could be the same thing that afflicted her crew. But there's no disease that could have come aboard. It's more like some kind of poisoning I've never seen before."

"Will he be all right?" Winthrop now asked, more concerned than scared.

"I've sedated him," Doyle replied. "I'll keep him in sick bay under observation until the laudanum wears off."

Moore was moved to Doyle's quarters. As the door clicked shut, Doyle sat at his side table. The ship groaned softly in the night punctuating Moore's breathing above the otherwise quiet sea.

Doyle leaned back in his chair, exhausted but alert. He pulled-out his pipe and watched his pipe smoke curling lazily around the room. He'd often prided himself on his ability to think through a problem, letting the facts fall into place like pieces of a puzzle.

Doyle cast a glance at the transcriptions from the *Octavius* logbook. The entries seemed to radiate a sinister presence in the smoke haze. Doyle thought, *I see the exact pattern of events in a cursed logbook, but don't know how they could be related, MacLeod said that taking it would bring nothing but pain and death, maybe he was right?*

Before long, Doyle's thoughts dissolved into smoke and he fell into a slumber.

The next morning, Moore claimed no knowledge of the events the previous day. He recalled only eating and having a smoke with the crew. Nobody else was affected and Doyle released Moore back to duty.

For lack of a better idea, Doyle gathered the crewmen that visited the *Octavius*. They sat around the table, their faces drawn and tired, haunted by the recent events. Li, Winthrop, MacLeod, Moore and Captain Garrett joined begrudgingly when they would have preferred to forget.

"We need to piece together everything that happened during our visit on the *Octavius*," said Doyle. "I need every detail, no matter how small."

Li, his hands folded in his lap, was the first to speak. "I tell everything already. No food left. All gone - eaten. I didn't get good look at cargo hold - Moore there. The ship too cold, too... dead."

Doyle nodded, but his eyes narrowed. "And the cargo markings, what did they mean?"

Li quickly shook his head. "I only saw glimpse. The symbols made no sense. Not seen before."

Doyle shifted his gaze to Winthrop, the midshipman. "You reported the dead bodies. Is there anything you didn't mention?"

Winthrop leaned back in his chair, his fingers tapping the table absently. "No. Just what I said before. Bodies, frozen solid, like they were ghosts themselves. A full ship, all dead."

"And the cargo?" Doyle pressed turning to Moore. "You said there were seeds and plants, things you didn't recognize. Did anything strike you as unusual?"

Moore scratched his head, frowning. "Aye, seeds or grain, and leaves.

"You said these botanicals were in barrels and cases in addition to bags. Is that unusual?" asked Doyle.

"I've never been in the spice trade. So, I don't know what's unusual," said Moore.

Before he could respond further, MacLeod, who had been sitting quietly, slammed his fist on the table. "Spirits!" he shouted, his voice thick with anger. "It was spirits-of-the-damned from *Octavius*. They came with us, with that cursed log."

Doyle glanced at him sharply. "We need facts we can use, not superstition. Besides, we returned the log."

MacLeod's eyes flashed with fury. "Here's the facts. *Octavius*' crew haunts us. The logbook brought their curse on board. It don't matter if it was returned."

"Well, the log's gone now," interjected Garret. "If yer right 'bout spirits, MacLeod, we can't be doin' nothin' now. Best let it go."

Doyle paused to let emotions subside, then began again. "All right, lets go deeper. There's some detail we missed..." There was a long silence with nobody wanting to revisit their time on the derelict.

"Ain't no use askin' more questions, Doyle," said Garret. "Nothin' to learn from it. We'll keep an eye on the crew and hope it's done with. But I'll have no more talk o' the *Octavius*."

Doyle was disappointed, but made no objection. Hopefully it was over.

Chapter
Silas

The crew returned to their tasks with new energy as the distance to the *Octavius* grew. By the time evening rolled around, all hands gathered in the galley for dinner. Banter filled the room as they passed around bread and fish. Doyle sat among them, quietly observing the crew's return to normal, his own mood improving with the festive atmosphere. He had his doubts about whether the troubles were truly over, but for now, the men were content. That was enough.

Silas was the last to enter and barely touched his food. The others were too engrossed in their conversation to notice at first, but Doyle, caught the subtle tremors in Silas's hands."Silas, you all right?"

For a moment, there was no reply. Then, Silas's lips began to move, forming words too faint for anyone to catch. The galley fell silent, the air thick with unease. Slowly, Silas raised his head, and his eyes wild, locked onto Doyle.

"They're... they're coming," he rasped. "We never left 'em behind. The *Octavius*... it followed us... waiting... in the ice."

"Silas," said Doyle. "We're safe. The lookouts would have reported any ship nearby. We're all alone."

Silas staggered to his feet, his gaze darting around the galley as if seeing specters. "They're here. They're all around us."

Doyle rose to try and calm Silas, but it was too late. Silas leaped over the table, knocking tin plates to the floor as he made a mad dash for the door. He flung it open, his muttering now an unintelligible jumble of desperation. Before anyone could pursue, he slammed the door shut and secured the storm hatch from the outside.

"Silas," Doyle called after him. He was already gone.

The crew, frozen in shock for a moment, sprang into action. Two tried to force the door, while the rest exited through the adjoining kitchen as Captain Garrett shouted orders. They frantically searched for Silas, but he remarkably disappeared into the night.

"Do you think he went overboard?" asked Baines.

"In these archaic waters' he'd already be dead," said Garret. "We assume he's alive until we find otherwise. Lads, keep searching."

Shortly thereafter, a call went up. Silas was found dead in the shadows, his body twisted at an odd angle. His eyes were open, but vacant, his chest still. Blood had pooled beneath him, staining the deck with a dark, wet sheen.

Doyle knelt beside the body and scanned for what killed him.

Captain Garrett leaned in, his face pale. "Is it the same... same as what done in the men on the *Octavius*?" he asked in a whisper.

"The one man had hung himself, so that's not exactly the same," said Doyle grimly. "However, the other man had the same contusion on his head."

Doyle turned to the gathered crew and asked if anybody saw what happened, everyone was silent. The new exuberance from the galley was gone and wouldn't soon return.

Chapter
Doyle's First Autopsy

Doyle returned to sickbay where Silas laid on the table. There was something particularly unsettling about the death of a fellow sailor, a man whose friendship he'd valued since he came aboard. Now, Silas was gone, leaving a void that felt more profound than the churning sea. He took a deep breath and began with a thorough examination of the body. He noted the pallor of his skin and the dark circles beneath his eyes. It was evident that Silas hadn't slept.

As he continued his inspection, Doyle noticed something unusual. There were small bruises on Jack's hands and face. "What happened to you, my friend?" Doyle murmured. "Were you swinging at specters and hurt yourself, or did these bruises come from somewhere else?"

He reached for his scalpel, carefully making the first incision down the middle of Silas' chest. The knife slid through the skin, parting flesh with a precision that belied the turmoil in his heart. The sight of the insides of the sailor's body sent a wave of nausea over him, but he pushed it aside, focused on the task at hand. As he opened the chest cavity, Doyle noted the telltale signs of overdose: the presence of darkened veins, a distinctive odor that hung in the air. It was unmistakable.

"You poor soul," he whispered, understanding flooding through him. Silas had been a victim of some insidious drug.

As Doyle continued his examination, he found signs of spasms in his muscles and an unusual rigidity. The combination of symptoms made him pause, his thoughts racing back to medical school. The deductive method he'd learned could unravel the most perplexing mysteries. *What if this wasn't merely a case of overdose ending in an accident?* Doyle's mind began to race. Silas wasn't a drinker and ate the same thing as everybody else. His only vice was caffeine and a smoke with the lads. Doyle struggled with many things…*How would drugs find their way into Silas, did he really know the man - was he an addict all along? Since his eyes were slightly dilated the day before, did some spectral vision cause him to seek escape through a drug, leading to the head injury? Did he obtain his bruises through a spasm before hitting his head, or were they the result of a struggle to stop from being drugged?*

As he finished his examination, Doyle was left more perplexed than before. If the death was more than just an accident; it wove a dark tapestry of fear, possibly murder, or even the supernatural. At this point in his medical career, he lacked the skills to know more.

Doyle debriefed Captain Garret on his findings. Doyle finished by saying, "That's all I could find from Silas' body. We'll have to turn elsewhere for more."

"Aye, I gotta gather his belongings to send off to his kin," said Garret. "Mebbe we can go through 'em together, see if there's anythin' that gives us a clue."

They located Silas' footlocker under his bunk in the forecastle. The musty scent of old cloth and saltwater filled the air as they carefully removed items from the battered box. Garrett held up a folded woolen blanket, frayed from years of use. Doyle extracted a well-worn Bible and a shaving kit. Beneath the usual sailor's belongings, Doyle found a sturdy boatswain's knife with its handle worn smooth from use. As they searched deeper,

Garrett's hand brushed against something hard and he lifted a carved whale tooth from the bottom of the chest. Holding it to the light, they could see it was still unfinished. However, it was far enough along to discern two children, a boy and a girl, their features remarkably similar.

"They look right proper together," Garret remarked, running his thumb over the scrimshaw. "Like they was twins, near enough."

Doyle nodded, then glanced at a photograph tucked under some clothes. "And here they are again," he said, holding up the image of the same children, their innocent faces frozen in time. "But I can't tell if they're Silas and a sibling, or his own children…"

Garret frowned, staring at the picture. "Hard to say. He were a quiet sort, fer all his friendliness. Never spoke a word 'bout either."

"I suppose the fact that he kept the photo and decided to spend his free time carving them into a keepsake meant they're special. We just don't know the exact relationship," observed Doyle setting the photo aside. The remainder of the chest yielded no other clues.

Garrett stared at the carved whale tooth still in his hand, while Doyle stood, gazing at the photograph of the children. They remained silent as they contemplated the loved ones now left behind.

"I don't know what done him in, Doyle," Garret said at last, his voice low and rough with weariness. "Whether it were some madness that took him or just a plain accident out there in the dark, I can't rightly say. But it feels like we lost him same as the crew o' the *Octavius*."

Doyle nodded, placing the photograph back into Silas's chest. "There's no telling for sure. The wound's familiar to the one sailor—eerily so—but we've no solid way of knowing if it's connected to the others. We weren't there when it happened. Could be an accident, but..." He trailed off, shaking his head.

Garret let out a deep sigh, his eyes fixed on the half-done carving in his hand. "Whatever it were, we're at a dead stop. We've gone through the man's things, an' none of it adds up. We can't dig no deeper, not while we're stuck on this ship."

Doyle looked out the small porthole, the endless sea dark against the horizon. "Every path we've followed leads back to the *Octavius*. Whatever answers we need are probably buried inside her."

Garrett stood, putting the whale tooth carefully back in the chest. "Aye. She's packed away in the ice and we'll never see her again, not in this lifetime."

Doyle gave a slow nod. "What do we do now?"

Garret stared hard at the sea chest. "We're paid to hunt whales, an' that's what we'll do. Keep the ship workin', keep her fishin'. But I'll tell ye this, Doyle—what happened here ain't somethin' I'll be forgettin'. Not me, an' not this crew."

England 1900
(the present)

Chapter
The Captain's Burden

The years had not been kind to Captain Garrett's cabin, nor to Garrett himself. The once neatly polished woodwork now bore the wear and tear of two decades at sea, and the captain's weathered face mirrored the ship's age. Doyle sat across from him, the same table where they had once examined the logbook entries was now uncharacteristically bare. A slow, uneasy silence hung between them, both men reflecting on the past.

"It's strange, ain't it?" Garrett finally said, staring into the dark brew in his mug. "After all this time, I still feel... guilty."

Doyle nodded slowly. "As do I. But we investigated it, Garrett. We searched for clues. We did everything we could."

Garrett sighed, rubbing a hand over his grizzled beard. "Aye, but we never knew for sure. Was it all just an accident? We stopped because the answers—" he trailed off, as though reluctant to speak of the ghost ship. "I figured Madame Seraphine would conjure up some vague spirits from the *Octavius* sayin' they'd moved on—nothin' more. Thought it'd keep the men busy 'til we got our pay in a few days."

"And yet, that night during the seance, Silas appeared. It wasn't just a hallucination or a trick of the mind. It was him— exactly as I remember him," said Doyle.

Garrett grunted in agreement. "He said his killer was in the room. Twenty years on, an' those words still haunt me. If it were murder, how come we didn't see it?"

Doyle shook his head. "I've been running his words through my mind. He said *'the guilty...here...'* Technically, we don't know if its one or more."

They both fell silent again, the weight of the revelations pressing down on them like the cold grip of the Arctic. Garrett broke the silence, his voice gruff but laced with uncertainty.

"Y'think... Madame Seraphine will call back Silas again? Maybe lay bare the guilty?"

Doyle's eyes narrowed as he considered the possibility. "If she's genuine, and if Silas was murdered, then yes, he might name his killer. But we have no way of knowing if Madame Seraphine is truly in touch with the dead or if it's all an elaborate performance."

Garrett nodded. "The men will be aboard for a few days yet. Once they're paid, we'll be on our way. In the meantime, you get with Madame Seraphine."

Doyle hesitated. "As you know from the newspapers, I've not been entirely successful discerning fact from fiction when dealing with these spiritualists."

"Yer the man who made Mr. Holmes. Surely, ye've got some o' the same cleverness."

"We better hope so..." said Doyle.

Chapter
Madame Seraphine

The day progressed with a sense of tension aboard the *Herald*. Though the fog had lifted slightly, the weight of the night's seance cast a shadow over the ship. Doyle contemplated the possibility of another seance to beckon Silas from the other side. Before too long, Seraphine climbed the gangplank and stood by the starboard railing. Her previous calm demeanor seemed frayed, and her gaze was distant.

"Good day, Madame," Doyle greeted her, offering a respectful nod. "It seems the ship awaits in excited anticipation of another evening of mysticism."

Seraphine turned to face him, her deep-set eyes glinting in the sunlight, but there was a tension behind her expression. "Indeed, Dr. Doyle, but anticipation is not all that fills the air today."

Doyle raised an eyebrow, catching the unease in her tone. "Something wrong?"

She hesitated, then reached into her cloak and pulled out a crumpled piece of paper. "I received this in my room this morning."

Doyle unfolded the note, the paper rough under his fingers. Scrawled in messy handwriting were the words: "*If you hold seance tonite, you will have a regret.*" The note had a spelling error and poor grammar, but the threat was clear.

"Charming," Doyle muttered, examining the note with a sharp eye. He brought it closer to his face, scrutinizing the ink and paper like the detective he'd so often written about.

Seraphine watched him, her lips twitching into a small smile. "What are you doing…attempting to channel your inner Holmes?"

Doyle didn't look up, but his mouth curved into a wry grin. "If I could channel a real Holmes, I would."

"So, what do you see?"

"The ink is smudged at the edges—likely a cheap quill, hurried writing. The paper itself is coarse, probably taken from ship supplies. And look here," he said pointing to a faint watermark, "this is not common writing parchment; it's closer to the stock we use aboard ship. Regardless, Silas death was no accident. Whoever wrote this note is the killer."

"So, Silas killer will be here tonight?"

"I believe so. Whoever wrote this didn't go to much trouble to conceal that fact. I assume it's not Captain Garret because his entries in the *Herald's* log are in a different hand."

"Unless the captain assumed you'd know that and is attempting misdirection."

"Yes, that's always possible. Whoever wrote this is obviously scared of being identified by Silas tonight."

She sighed, her previous amusement fading. "Someone vigorously believes that I can unleash the truth."

"Can you?"

"I'm not sure," she admitted, her voice quieter now. "But whoever wrote this thinks I can. And I fear that tonight may be more dangerous than I anticipated."

Doyle studied her face, sensing the depth of her concern. Despite her usual confident demeanor, there was a real fear in her eyes. He leaned in slightly, his tone turning warm. "We could cancel it. Investigate further before…"

"No," she interrupted, shaking her head. "If we stop now, we may never get another chance."

Doyle crossed his arms, torn between caution and the undeniable pull of the mystery. "The seance may bring the answers we've been searching for, but what if it doesn't...what if it brings danger instead?"

Seraphine met his gaze, her voice steady. "I'm not convinced we will find the answer tonight. However, I am convinced that we *won't* if we cancel. If there is danger, we face it. The truth is often precarious, but we cannot hide from it."

Doyle ran a hand through his hair, the weight of the situation pressing down on him. "Very well, then. But promise me, Madame, you will be cautious. Threats like these—misspelling or not—are not to be taken lightly."

She nodded, though her expression remained resolute. "I have no intention of dying tonight, Dr. Doyle."

Doyle tucked the note into his pocket, glancing out at the vast sea beyond that harbor. "Then we'll proceed with me sitting next to you the entire time," he said finally, his voice firm. "If anything seems off during the seance, we stop. Agreed?"

"Agreed," Seraphine replied, though there was a flicker of uncertainty in her eyes.

As the sun took its course across the sky, they stood together. It felt natural for Doyle. He wondered if the Madame felt the same.

Chapter
Second Seance

Twilight's arrival found Doyle standing at the entrance to the galley. Each participant bore a haunted look, shadows of their pasts etched into their faces.

Madame Seraphine, moved gracefully around the room, her presence both captivating and unsettling. She had changed into a flowing gown of deep blue, reminiscent of the ocean, with intricate silver embroidery that shimmered like starlight.

Doyle observed her keenly. If she was afraid, she certainly didn't show it. He could see the reason for her stage success. They extinguished the gas lamps adorning the space before leaving the room lit by a single flickering candle in the table's center. The former crew were seated in their original places with their faces barely illuminated. Doyle took a seat next to Seraphine's spot, his pulse quickening as he prepared for what was to come.

Seraphine took her place at the head of the table. The familiar weight of the past pressed down on everyone, but tonight felt different—darker, more foreboding.

"I remind you all," she began, her voice steady but tight, "Silas promised to name the one responsible for his death. But I must warn you, the spirit world is unpredictable. Sometimes the veil between us is thick."

Doyle's fingers fidgeted with his sleeve, betraying his nervousness. The rest of the crew exchanged uneasy glances, their faces pale.

Seraphine placed her hands on the table, palms down, and closed her eyes. "Silas, if you can hear us, come forward. We are seeking the truth and only you hold the key."

A long silence followed, broken only by the gentle groan of the ship's timbers. Madame Seraphine shifted in her seat, her face tightening with concentration. The moments dragged on, painfully slow.

"Silas, speak to us," she urged, her voice louder now. "We are waiting."

Still nothing.

The room seemed to grow colder, the air tingling with an electric tension, but no spirit appeared. The single lamp flickered, casting its dim light over their faces, as Seraphine pushed harder.

"Silas," she said, almost pleading now. "You said you would return. What holds you back?"

A faint shimmer began to form in the corner of the room, barely perceptible at first, like a mist curling up from the shadows. Seraphine's breath caught in her throat. Silas gradually materialized before them. His figure was barely there, ghostly and indistinct, like an outline drawn in fog. He stood silent.

"Silas..." Seraphine pressed, leaning toward the apparition. "You said you'd return to name your killer. Why are you not speaking?"

Silas's ghost stood eerily erect as before, his form flickering like a dying flame. His eyes, hollow and distant, seemed to gaze at something far away—something they couldn't see. When he finally spoke through Seraphine, his voice was slow and distant, as if coming from the bottom of the sea.

"The *Octavius*…it brought the darkness to the surface."

Silas was silent again. The seconds stretched unbearably, the tension in the room mounting with each breath. Seraphine's own voice returned, her patience wearing thin. "Silas, please. You must be clearer. Who killed you? Who was driven to it?"

100

A long, agonizing pause followed. Then, slowly, Silas spoke again through her. "The guilty...already tainted...long before the *Octavius*. It... only... brought them out."

Doyle leaned forward his voice tight with frustration. "Who? Silas, who? You need to tell us—"

Before he could finish, there was a loud clatter against the wall that made everyone jump and turn. Then, the center lamp was snuffed out - plunging the room into total darkness. There was movement jarring the table and Madame Seraphine screamed.

Doyle placed his arms around her in a protective hug. He could hear the others moving frantically in the room, their panic rising as they scrambled to make sense of the sudden attack. The hiss of gas filled the room as somebody managed to light the wall lamps. Madame Seraphine clutched her face, her cheeks were red where struck by something. The others stood scattered around the room, their eyes wide with surprise.

"Nobody move," Doyle shouted, though his own nerves were frayed. "What happened?"

"I was struck in the darkness. I thought I was in danger," she said her voice shaky. "I think my scream stopped them."

Doyle scanned the floor and table. There was no weapon. He looked at the crew standing throughout the compartment. "Who attacked Madame Seraphine?"

The room went silent.

Chapter
Doyle Returns Seraphine

Doyle guided Seraphine through the dimly lit streets, the tension of the seance still buzzing between them. She clung to his arm, visibly shaken by the attack. The cold Whitby air bit at their faces as they approached her inn above a pub.

They entered and selected a quiet corner of the bar. Doyle ordered two brandies, hoping the strong drink would settle them both. Seraphine sat quietly, her fingers still trembling. Doyle placed the glass in front of her and raised his own in a small toast. "Here's to settling our nerves," he said gently, offering her a faint smile.

She took a sip, the amber liquid warming her throat. For a moment, neither spoke, letting the tension between them subside. Doyle watched her, wondering how to begin. Finally, he leaned forward, his voice low but firm. "I must say, Madame, the appearance of Silas tonight was—well, he looked real. But you'll forgive me if I'm cautious. I've been tricked before."

Seraphine looked up at him, her eyes dark and unreadable. "You're referring to the Cottingley Fairies, aren't you?"

Doyle hesitated. He hadn't expected her to bring it up so directly. "Yes. It was... a painful lesson. I believed those photographs were real, that they offered proof of something extraordinary."

Her eyes softened and she set her glass down, leaning in slightly. "I read the editorials that skewered your name. Your intentions were pure."

Doyle's heart twisted. She spoke as if she felt his humiliation. "It was a mistake, and I've learned from it. What happened tonight… Silas or whatever we saw, was vague. If he had come back to name his killer, why so evasive?"

Seraphine stared into her glass, her voice barely above a whisper. "Perhaps because some truths are too painful to speak. Or perhaps the veil between the worlds is not so easily parted. Silas will have his justice—whether through the living or the dead. If the killer admits their guilt, that's all that matters."

Doyle raised an eyebrow, the skepticism creeping back into his mind. "So you're saying it doesn't matter if Silas's appearance was staged or real. As long as justice is served, by whatever means available, it doesn't matter."

She met his gaze, her expression unreadable. "Justice isn't always as clear-cut as we'd like it to be. But what matters is that the truth comes to light."

He frowned, swirling the brandy in his glass. "I'm not sure what you're admitting, if anyting, Madame."

She tilted her head, curiosity flickering across her face. "Tell me, Dr. Doyle. What *did* happen in the Arctic?"

Doyle sighed. It was a convenient change of subject, but still a valid query. "Twenty years ago, aboard the *Herald,* we found the derelict *Octavius,* drifting in the Arctic. Her crew was frozen to death—every last one of them." Doyle briefly summarized the log entries, disposition of the *Octavius* at Baffin Island, strange crew behavior that followed and the death of Silas. He concluded saying, "We couldn't tell if Silas's death was an accident, or murder. We did what investigation we could, but to no avail."

Seraphine leaned forward, "How hard did you try?"

"We expelled every talent we had," Doyle said slightly defensive.

She nodded slowly, her expression thoughtful. "Then perhaps it's time to investigate again. But this time, you won't be alone. I'll help you. Together, we'll uncover what really happened —whether the answers lie with the living *or* the dead."

Doyle gazed at her, uncertainty swirling in his chest. She was enigmatic, frustratingly so, but there was something about her, a determination he found difficult to resist.

"You're serious?" he asked, a hint of caution in his voice.

"Very," she replied, her gaze unwavering. "You've already seen that the past is not so easily buried. If we work together, we may finally bring Silas, and the rest of them, peace. Isn't that worth the effort?"

Doyle drained the last of his brandy, feeling the warmth spread throughout. The skepticism in his mind still whispered caution. If she had a hidden agenda, she could discredit him further.

"All right," he said finally. "It's safer than a seance because we'll be together. But I need your honesty. No more evasion. If we're going to do this, we do it properly."

She smiled, a flicker of amusement in her eyes. "Agreed, Doctor. I wouldn't have it any other way."

After some additional discussion, they decided that she would be safe in her locked room at the inn until retrieved by Doyle each day. The killer had no reason to pursue her with no additional seance.

Chapter
New Investigation

Doyle and Seraphine stepped into Captain Garret's cramped cabin. Garret stood, arms crossed, his gaze intense as he eyed them both. After the unsettling events of the previous evening, he was clearly uneasy.

Garret cleared his throat. "I'll cut to it—are you planning another seance?"

Doyle shook his head. "Not now, Captain. Not until we investigate first. I don't want to put Madame Seraphine at further risk until we've exhausted other avenues. I think a more investigate approach could prove just as useful. We'll start by speaking with each crewman individually. We'll get a complete account of their experiences on the *Octavius*."

"We already did that 20 years ago," countered Garret.

"Twenty years ago we didn't know it was murder. Now we do and know what questions to ask."

Garret sat in silence trying to process it all. Seraphine took the opportunity to reinforce the point. "Silas wasn't as forthcoming in the last seance as we hoped. The only thing for sure is that it triggered action by the murderer. If we can find his identity through normal investigation, we won't have to resort to triggering another attack in the dark."

"Fine. You can start your investigation with me," offered Garret. He pointed for Doyle and Seraphine to take two seats.

"I remember that day clear as if it were yesterday," Garret began, his voice steady but heavy, like a weight he couldn't shake. "Doyle an' me, we were among the first to board the *Octavius*. Eerie it was—dead quiet. The whole crew, frozen stiff like statues, each in their place, the cold preservin' 'em as they were. The captain, he was still sat in his cabin, clutchin' the ship's log like it were a lifeline. We searched through his log entries, hopin' for answers, but all we found was madness in them last lines—talk of strange behavior among the crew and death all 'round. There was somethin' desperate in those words, like he knew what was comin', but couldn't escape it."

"It also had some references to the king and a mountain," added Doyle. "The references were probably part of the madness growing among the captain and crew."

Garret nodded in agreement, then continued. "When we left the *Octavius*, the *Herald's* crew weren't the same—strange they were, withdrawn-like. Silas, now he never stepped foot aboard the *Octavius*, was the first to show any signs. Came to Doyle, said he was feelin' a bit muddled in the head. Not long after, Moore—another crewman—had himself a violent turn, one Doyle had to step in an' fix."

"What do you mean fix?" asked Seraphine.

"I administered laudanum. He didn't remember anything of the incident the next day."

"What happened next Captain Garret?" asked Seraphine returning her gaze to him.

"Then Silas started seein' things in the galley, rantin' like a madman. He bolted outta there, screamin' his head off. We found him dead with a wound to his skull. We reckon now it weren't no accident."

Seraphine turned again to Doyle, her expression focused. "Could you have administered laudanum in the galley and saved him?"

"There wasn't time. It happened too fast."

108

"What can you tell me about Silas himself. His background —anything that might help us understand him?" continued Seraphine.

Garret rubbed his chin, recalling. "We know little of Silas. He went to sea as a 12 year old. He never spoke of his kin. He was steady enough when he signed on. After the *Octavius*... something changed."

"When you say *changed*, you mean his strange behavior culminating in his death?"

"Yes," said Garret without elaboration turning to Doyle for assistance.

"I have nothing to add," said Doyle. "Since I was with Captain Garret most of the time, his testimony is the same as my own. All I can say is that it is completely accurate."

They discussed a few details of Silas condition with Seraphine to satisfy her curiosity, then concluded their meeting and went in search of another crewman.

110

Chapter
Baines Interview

The two made their way to Baines' quarters amidships, noting the cramped space filled with the smell of salt, wood, and stale tobacco. He looked up as they entered, tipping his cap atop ruffled gray hair, with a wary glance. His quarters were sparsely decorated and carried a quiet sense of routine that suggested a man accustomed to keeping to himself.

Doyle explained their presence and began with a straightforward question. "We know you weren't on the *Octavius* when we made our expedition, Baines. But you were close with the crew and might help anyway—did you know Silas well?"

Baines considered this, his eyes narrowing slightly as he looked back on their time together. "Silas was a good lad.Young, eager, liked to prove himself. We'd share a smoke on deck now and again between watches. It helped keep the chill off. He was a hard worker, Silas. Had his superstitions, but what sailor doesn't?"

"What superstitions?" asked Seraphine.

"You know, the normal stuff we all follow...never set sail on a Friday—bad luck on account of Christ's crucifixion. Don't whistle aboard a ship because it calls up the wind - not the kind you want."

Seraphine fought the urge to chuckle and continued. "And your time before the *Herald*, Mr. Baines? We know you came from the spice trade. Did you ever handle any of the shipments, like those on the *Octavius*?"

Baines' posture stiffened just slightly. "I'm a sailmaker and didn't deal with the cargo much. My work was with the sails and rigging, not crates and barrels. I kept to myself, same as most."

"Getting back to Silas, did you have any conflict, it's a small ship and people must get on each other's nerves?" asked Seraphine.

"Like I said, I'm a sailmaker. I kept to myself."

There was a guardedness in his answer that Seraphine mentally noted, something almost dismissive in how he glossed over his past and interaction with Silas. It was hard to determine if he was that introverted, or kept to himself for some reason.

Before they left, Doyle asked a final question. "Did Silas ever mention his family or seem troubled by something personal? Perhaps a memory or an experience that unsettled him?"

Baines thought for a moment, shaking his head. "Silas was nice enough, but private. I was surprised he whittled what appeared to be family on the whale tooth. I heard the lads say they were probably kids he didn't want to talk about because the wife took them. You know how it is for sailors on voyages that last for months or years. Their families move-on, sometimes because they have to find another man to support them."

There seemed little to gain from the sailmaker, so they moved-on.

Chapter
Moore Interview

Doyle and Seraphine found Richard Moore in his small quarters near the cargo hold. The shelves around him, once crowded with supplies, ledger books, and spilt whale oil, now sat empty. Moore, appeared even more grizzled now the he reached his late fifties. Despite a guarded expression, he gestured for them to sit. After a brief exchange of pleasantries, they dove into the heart of the matter.

"Moore, we'd like to discuss the cargo hold on the *Octavius*. You mentioned seeds and leaves with Chinese markings. Tell us about it," said Seraphine.

Moore scratched his head, his gaze drifting. "That's all it was—some kind of botanicals, seeds mostly, packed in burlap sacks with labels I couldn't read. Can't say I've ever seen anything like them."

"I thought they were also in barrels and crates?" interjected Seraphine.

"Yes. Barrels and crates - all with the same label in Chinese. That's how I know they were botanicals, the same label," responded Moore.

"Is it normal?" asked Doyle. "To carry the same cargo in such diverse containers?"

"I wouldn't know," shrugged Moore. "I suppose they used what containers they could get. Like I said, they had the same labels as the bag I opened."

"Did you bring samples of any of the cargo back with you?" asked Seraphine.

"No, ma'am," he replied casually. "Didn't see a reason to, not from that cursed ship. I wasn't about to take a thing from her."

Doyle noticed a slight unease in Moore's manner. They pressed several more questions about the cargo, but got nowhere.

"Was anyone else in the hold with you? Any strange noises or signs someone else might've been down there?" asked Seraphine.

Moore hesitated, glancing down at his hands. "The years may be playing tricks with my memory. I've even dreamed in my sleep about that day over the years. So, it's hard to separate fact from fancy. But I vaguely recall that I heard something down there, a sort of shuffling sound. I called out, thought maybe it was one of the landing party - but there was no answer, just an echo."

Seraphine leaned in, her tone softer but probing. "We understand you experienced strange visions, just like Silas, that turned violent. Is it possible that you shared a meal or a drink with him before these visions began?"

Baines glanced between them, his expression growing contemplative. "Aye, of course," he replied, scratching his stubbled chin. "All of us shared the same food from the galley. Li—the cook —he'd sometimes surprise us, especially on night watches. Hand out sweet buns, a bit of rum if we were lucky. Just to lift the spirits on those long stretches in the dark."

Seraphine nodded thoughtfully. "But only the two of you experienced the strange visions. How could that be?"

"Don't rightly know," shrugged Moore.

"And the spice trade? Did you have any previous experience there?" asked Seraphine.

Moore shook his head. "No, ma'am, none at all. I'd have no clue what those cargo markings even meant. The botanicals were way beyond my knowledge."

After a pause, Doyle turned to Moore. "Tell us about your relationship with Silas. Any troubles between the two of you?"

Moore grimaced, a hint of irritation flashing across his face. "Silas... well, he wasn't the easiest of fellows. We had a bit of a row after he accused me of skimming from the stores and passing off bad meat. Claimed I was taking from the supply budget for myself."

"Were you?" Doyle asked, his voice even, though his gaze held a hint of challenge.

"Not a bit of truth in it," Moore replied firmly, eyes narrowing. "It's common, you see, with lads like, Silas. Everyone's got something to say about the storekeeper, especially when they think rations are too lean or the meat's gone foul. Comes with the territory."

Doyle leaned back, scrutinizing Moore's expression. "So, you've had similar accusations from others?"

Moore nodded, shrugging off the implication. "Aye, always something. But I keep the books right, make sure the lads get what's allotted. Silas wasn't more vocal than anyone else."

After wrapping up their questions, Doyle and Seraphine took their leave. Moore's recounting of his time in the *Octavius'* hold, the phantom noises, and the accusations from Silas lingered in their thoughts.

115

116

Chapter
Winthrop Interview

They found Midshipman Winthrop in the dimly lit cabin he'd taken forward of his old quarters, a step-up from his original lodgings. He obviously felt entitled for an upgrade after briefly owning the *Herald* on the death of his father.

Winthrop regarded them with a flicker of wariness and nodded as they entered. He looked slightly out of place in his elegant suit of clothes bought with what they assumed were the final remnants of his squandered inheritance. After taking their seats, Doyle began with a straightforward question.

"Winthrop, you were one of the few to enter the *Octavius* with us. What can you tell Madame Seraphine about what you found?"

Winthrop's face softened. "Captain Garret and yourself had taken the main quarters, while I was tasked with the cabins. There I found the woman and her child—both long dead, frozen in their beds. Other crewman lay frozen in the other quarters the same way. Two others were under a canvas that you examined. After seeing the state of those poor souls, I left quickly. Didn't stay long enough to look at anything else."

Doyle nodded, recalling the sorrowful scene himself. Shifting his line of inquiry, he continued, "There was an incident on the *Herald*. You were the first to find Moore violently hallucinating. Can you tell us anything more about that?"

Winthrop shook his head, his brow creasing with lingering disbelief. "We were sharing a smoke. He had his pipe and I had mine. Then he went crazy and started yelling. He locked himself in the deck house and then you appeared."

"Were you close friends?" asked Seraphine. "Did you always smoke together?"

"No, we weren't friends at all. In fact, that was probably the first time we smoked together. He thought me a 'spoiled boy,' called me lazy now and again - like the others. They'd mutter about my father's influence, how I got by easy on board," his expression hardened.

"You said the others called you spoiled. Did that include Silas?" asked Seraphine,

"I suppose so."

"Did you ever do anything about it?" asked Doyle.

"If you mean, did I kill him, the answer is no. If I wanted him gone, I'd have him fired after taking ownership of the ship from by father. You see, people in my class don't need to kill. We have other means of dealing with our subordinates. I wouldn't expect you to understand."

Doyle ignored that barb, but decided to needle him with his next question none-the-less. "After the *Herald*'s return, what came of you and your family's ownership in the *Herald*?"

Winthrop snorted, his face turning slightly red. "Everyone knows I had to sell her years ago. My gambling debts piled up, and she was the first thing to go when I got my inheritance. Any hope of profiting from her, well, that's long gone. There's nothing left for me to gain from the *Herald*'s past. The only thing I have is a bad memory, for whatever that's worth."

After a couple more questions, Doyle and Seraphine rose to leave. Winthrop's answers were filed away as another thread in the growing tangle of mysteries surrounding the *Octavius* and *Herald*. Each story, each conflict, hinted at resentments that had simmered beneath the surface.

Chapter

Li Interview

Doyle and Seraphine made their way to the ship's galley where the Li stirred a bubbling pot of stew. The rich aroma of meat and herbs filled the cramped space, a stark contrast to the foreboding atmosphere that surrounded the investigations. The cook looked up as they entered, his brow furrowing slightly at the sight of them.

"Good day, Mr. Li," Doyle greeted him, stepping forward. "By now, you've probably heard from the others that we were coming. We have some questions regarding your time on the *Octavius*."

The cook nodded slowly, wiping his hands on a rag before leaning against the counter. "Words move fast on small ship."

Seraphine looked questioning at Doyle and Li. "I didn't see anybody leave their quarters after we spoke. How did word get here?"

Doyle and Li chuckled. "On ships, scuttlebutt can make it from one end to the other in ways defying all laws of physics, my dear." He then turned to Li to begin. "So, what can you tell us about your visit to the *Octavius*?"

"I checked the kitchen and pantry on other ship. No food, only dust." Li shrugged, a look of resignation crossing his face. "Nothing to cook. Nothing to eat for them. All die."

Doyle exchanged a glance with Seraphine before continuing, "I seem to recall you were late returning to the boat. What held you back?"

His brow furrowed deeper. "My English... not so good. I no understand the call to leave. It was noisy, and I was in kitchen. I thought I had time," he replied, his accent thick as he struggled to convey his thoughts.

Doyle hesitated knowing it was hardly noisy in the *Octavius* kitchen. If anything, it was quiet as the grave. However, he let it pass.

"Prior to working on the *Herald*, what kind of ship were you on?" Seraphine asked.

"I was on river junks, then moved to a whaling ship, not the spice trade as you ask everyone," he explained, stirring the pot absentmindedly.

Doyle thought to himself, s*cuttlebutt is one thing, but already knowing each question before we arrived is another.* He shifted the conversation. "What about your relationships with the crew, particularly, Silas and Moore?"

Li shook his head vehemently. "No relationship. They make fun of my Chinese, and food, but... so does everyone. Just part of life for all foreign cooks."

"Did you ever get mad, like at Silas for example?" pushed Seraphine.

Li seemed about to divulge something, but held back. He said simply, "No. I just cook."

After a pause, Seraphine asked, "Do you have family, Mr. Li?"

"No family. I work on boats since I was boy. The *Herald* is family now." Li subconsciously touched the rib of the ship next to the stove.

"How do you feel about the ship being scrapped?"

"Like all of us, ship must die before too long," said Li looking down.

Seraphine decided to switch tack. "You mentioned previously to Doyle that the Chinese symbol on the cargo made no sense..."

"It was not Chinese Hanzi writing," said Li without elaboration.

After a couple more questions that received vague answers, Doyle signaled that they should leave.

"Thank you, Mr. Li," Doyle said rising with a smile. "I for one always enjoyed your cooking. I speak of it fondly to this day."

Li gave a simple nod as they left.

As they walked, Seraphine asked Doyle. "What do you think about Li's answers regarding the cargo symbol and words with Silas?"

"I think he knows more than he's letting on," said Doyle. "His comment about the Hope 'dying' also seemed strange. It could be because of his struggle with English, or something more..."

Chapter
MacLeod Interview

Doyle and Seraphine made their way to the boatswain's locker where the Chief Boatswain MacLeod was tending to lines that needed no tending. His grizzled beard and hair looked more unkempt than normal.

"I was wondering when you'd get around to me," MacLeod said sarcastically.

"Saved the best for last," said Seraphine with an awkward smile.

Doyle sat on a large coiled line and signaled for Seraphine to do the same.

"We'll start with your time on the *Octavius*," he said making no attempt at smalltalk, his lack of fondness for MacLeod on full display.

"Aye, I can tell you what I saw. But there ain't much to tell. I stayed near the whaleboat, preparing it for our return. Spent most of my time on the upper weather deck checking lines and spars. The *Octavius* was seaworthy when we got there, as far as I could tell. But then you'all returned, and we pushed-off. Nothing more to it."

Seraphine leaned forward, and jumped to the question possibly linking her as a spiritualist, to MacLeod. "You objected to taking the *Octavius'* log. Why?"

MacLeod's expression darkened. "You know better than most that them spirits are linked to their items. It ain't no different with sailors. Nothing good would come from keeping it on *Herald*." MacLeod's last comment came with an aggressive stare at Doyle who glared back in return.

Sensing the tension, Seraphine tried to leverage whatever connection she and MacLeod shared by continuing. "You are a credit to those in my profession, Mr. MacLeod. Few people have an awareness of the spiritual world. Have you any other experiences we can learn from?"

MacLeod turned back his gaze as if debating whether she was sincere. He decided in her favor. "I know the spirits deceive just as they do in life. Silas died from an accident, I'm sure of it. You're stirring things up that ought to be left alone."

Seraphine countered gently. "Yes, its true that spirits can lie. But they can also tell the truth. Either way, we owe it to Silas to understand what truly happened. There are still questions that need answering."

MacLeod shook his head vehemently. "No more seances, no more poking around. Some things are better left in the past."

Doyle interjected, trying to maintain a diplomatic tone. "We understand your concerns, MacLeod, but Silas deserves justice."

MacLeod exhaled sharply, his frustration evident. "You may think you're doing right, but it could end in more pain. I won't be a part of it - and I'm not the only one. Me and the lads all agree that we leave when we get our £100 and the ship gets towed. Be damned with your investigation."

With that, MacLeod abruptly stood, ending the conversation. Doyle and Seraphine exchanged glances, recognizing nothing more was to be gained and left.

"He seemed extremely aggressive," observed Seraphine. "Is he always like that?"

"Not always," replied Doyle. "He seemed agitated more than usual. We may yet have another crack at him."

"We're running out of time and people to question…" said Seraphine with concern.

Doyle sensed uncharacteristic desperation in her voice. "There's nothing more to be gained from the crew today. Let's walk in the direction of the inn and determine what to do next."

Chapter
Tea Time

On the way to the inn, Doyle suggested that a change of scenery might be helpful and suggested a local tea house. A short walk found a quaint establishment tucked away in a narrow side street where the cacophony of the harbor faded into a soft murmur. The air inside was warm and fragrant, filled with the comforting scent of freshly brewed tea and baked goods. Doyle chose a secluded corner table, hoping the atmosphere would clear their thoughts.

He held out a seat for Seraphine, then settled himself. She smoothed her skirts and placed her hands on the table. The warmth of the room contrasted sharply with the chill that still gripped her, a reminder of the darkness surrounding them.

"Thank you for enjoying tea with me, Madame" Doyle began, while she poured steaming tea into delicate porcelain cups.

She nodded, her eyes reflecting a mix of gratitude. "I appreciate it, Doctor. This place feels... safe. It's a respite from the unpleasantness."

Doyle took a sip of his tea, savoring the rich flavor before continuing. "The crew interviews haven't yielded anything more than I already knew. Is there another line of inquiry we should be trying?"

Seraphine pondered the question for a moment. "Perhaps we should begin by focusing why on the *Octavius* deviated from her course to brave the Northwest Passage. You mentioned that they attempted a suicidal route through the unknown passage when professional explorers before them had failed."

"That's correct. I've always wondered if it was linked to the strange log reference regarding '*the drive of Thistle Mountain.*' You think they're related?"

"Maybe. You assumed that the reference seemed too small a motivation to attempt the passage. I would concur, especially given the presence of the captain's wife and son on the ship. A reference to visiting some place presumably linked to home wouldn't justify the almost suicidal route. Can Thistle Mountain mean something else?"

"Over the years, I've made small inquiries regarding the place," said Doyle shaking his head. "Given that no such place exists in all of England, or even Europe for that matter. I assumed it was some small hill of the captain's childhood."

"That may be so. However, that still leaves insufficient motivation to take such a journey. Was there anything else in the log?"

"The only other reference to a possible motivation was the entry regarding '*disappointing My King.*'"

"Is that the King of England?" asked Seraphine refilling their teas.

"I don't know. If the crown needed transport of something of national importance, they would not have chosen a whaling ship. I assume they'd use the Royal Navy. A sloop of war could have easily been acquired from the base in Hong Kong. It would also have been faster."

"What other king is there, then. Christ the King?" asked Seraphine. "Was there any religious icons in the captain's cabin to indicate he was a spiritual man?"

"None that I recall. So you think the belief in some divine appointment could drive him to seek the Northwest Passage when none succeeded before?"

"I don't know. Could the two references be related. Is Thistle Mountain the title of some lessor known religious order and The King, their overseer?"

"I'm aware of a prominent theological school not far from here. I assume we can find a professor with knowledge of any such order. What about some *less Christian* search? Thistle Mountain has an enchanted ring to it."

"My friend, Eleanor, is a member of the Ancient Order of Druids and coincidentally has a bookshop in Whitby. If anyone has knowledge of a Thistle Mountain or the king of such a sacred place, she'll likely know of them. We can go there straight away."

"Let's just hope that Thistle Mountain isn't some reference to the captain's favorite pub..."

Chapter
Eleanor

The bell above the door chimed softly as Seraphine and Doyle stepped into the dimly lit confines of the spiritual bookstore. The scent of old parchment and incense filled the air, enveloping them in an exotic embrace. Bookshelves lined the walls, crammed with volumes on mysticism, spirituality, and the occult, their spines faded and worn from years of handling. Soft, ethereal music played on a phonograph adding to the store's mystical atmosphere.

They made their way through the narrow aisles, occasionally brushing their fingers against the textured spines of the tomes. Doyle soaked-in titles like, *The Secrets of Mother Earth*.

"Eleanor," Seraphine called out, her voice warm and inviting as she rounded a corner.

Eleanor, a petite woman with silver-streaked hair and an enigmatic smile, emerged from the back room, her arms laden with various iconic merchandise. She dropped them onto a nearby table and beamed at Seraphine. "My dear! It's so lovely to see you. And, who might you be then?"

"I'm sorry," said Seraphine. "Let me introduce you to Dr. Doyle."

Doyle shook her hand firmly, his expression one of curiosity. "It's a pleasure, Eleanor."

"I'm so sorry about your troubles with the Cottingley Fairies. Just because two schoolgirls played a prank doesn't mean that fairies don't exist. I hope you're still a believer..."

"I'm certainly open to the possibilities," said Doyle sheepishly.

The three moved to three chairs by two windows normally reserved for readers. "I sense a troubling aura around you both. How can I help?"

"Eleanor, we have a problem," said Seraphine with a serious tone. She then described the encounter with the *Octavius* and the mysterious log entries describing *Thistle Mountain* and M*y King*. Eleanor listened wide eyed. As the story progressed, she became almost giddy. At the end, she responded at length.

"To understand Druid beliefs, one must understand their connection to the earth," she began, her eyes brightening. "To the Druids, the earth isn't just a resource. It's a living, breathing entity — the essence of life itself. We believe every stone, tree, river, and mountain is infused with spirit and wisdom. Ancient Druids would say the earth is a vast, sacred text, with every hill and valley holding secrets."

"Could Thistle Mountain be a place holding secrets?" asked Doyle. In truth, he was deeply familiar with Druidism, but listened patiently to Eleanor's description before guiding the conversation to the unknown site.

"It could. There are places in the British Isles that are particularly sacred. These locations are believed to possess a unique energy — an alignment, if you will, with the rhythms of nature and the cosmos. I'm sure you're aware of Stonehenge…"

"Of course," replied Doyle.

"Other lessor known places are *Avebury* in Wiltshire, for instance. The ancient stone circle there is even older than Stonehenge. It's said to mark a center of immense spiritual power, a crossroads of energies that connect earth and sky."

"Why stones in particular?" asked Doyle. "Could stones include natural rock formations on mountains?"

Eleanor gestured with her hands to the view of nature out the window. "The stones themselves hold the memory of the earth. According to Druid beliefs, they are like the guardians of time, and by arranging them in circles, they draw in energy from the cosmos, creating a space where past, present, and future can be seen as one. *Glastonbury Tor* in Somerset is another sacred place. The hill is topped by a tower and is known as a gateway to the Otherworld, the spiritual realm. Those are just two."

Seraphine smiled. "So, a higher elevation may be a corridor to the Otherworld.   Have you heard of Thistle Mountain as a sacred place?"

"No," replied Eleanor with visible disappointment. "However, that doesn't mean its not one to some Druid group. Many places are special to a local Druid community. Let me reach out to some of our groves. That's what we call our local gathering groups - groves, like a tree grove. Somebody will know if there is such a place in England, or even possibly Europe."

Doyle then described the symbol found on the *Octavius* cargo. Eleanor wasn't familiar, but made a sketch to add to her inquiries. With that, Doyle and Seraphine agreed to come back in a couple days.

Chapter
MacLeod's Body

The frigid evening air bristled as Doyle walked back from the Inn where he left Seraphine for the evening. The *Herald's* silhouette was marked by the light of gas lanterns inside a a dim gray haze as he approached the waterfront. A huddle of men stood near the center mast, their faces looking aloft with confusion. Captain Garret was among them, his voice strained as he yelled, "MacLeod! Fer heaven's sake, man, get yerself down. Ain't no one after ye — it's all in yer head."

Doyle followed their gazes upward, squinting to make out the figure of Chief Boatswain MacLeod clinging to the crow's nest high above. His face was a pale mask of terror, his hands gripping the ropes in white-knuckled desperation.

"What's happening?" Doyle asked. "I just saw him a few hours ago and he was fine."

Before Garret could answer, MacLeod's voice rang out, hoarse and fractured, barely audible over the murmurs below. "From the *Octavius*...they've come for me. I won't be dragged into their cursed abyss."

"MacLeod!" Doyle shouted, his voice calm but firm, hoping to cut through the man's panic. "There are *no* demons, you hear? You're safe. We're all here to help you."

MacLeod's head moved back and forth as if he was watching spirits on either end of the yardarm.

"You don't understand! You never did, Doyle."

"MacLeod, that's enough!" Garret tried again, using his authoritative command voice. "Come down now..."

135

A silence stretched between them, and for a brief moment, it seemed MacLeod might relent. He shifted his weight, gripping the stays attached to the mast and glanced down. But just as quickly, his face contorted into fear once more, as though he saw something only he could perceive.

"No," he screamed.

Before anyone could react, MacLeod's hands released the lines, and he plunged downward, his scream swallowed by the mist. The crew flinched as he struck the deck with a sickening thud, lifeless before their eyes. A stunned silence followed, broken only by the nervous whispers that echoed MacLeod's final word.

Doyle clenched his jaw, a chilling unease settling over him. *This could be no accident. Whatever had driven MacLeod to madness was far more insidious than mere superstition.*

Captain Garret knelt, his face pale and grim as he whispered,"If this don't end soon, we'll all be dead, sure as the tide."

Chapter
Local Constabulary

Doyle explained MacLeod's death to the local detective Edwin Mulligan as he leaned over the body on deck. "I understand it may look like a tragic fall," Doyle said, "but it's more than that. This man was plagued with visions—haunted by what he believed were specters from a derelict ship encounter long ago. We held a seance to contact another sailor who died there years ago, one Silas..."

Detective Sergeant Mulligan, a broad-shouldered man with a thick black mustache, raised a hand to silence him.

"Hold on, Doctor," his eyes glinted with an amused spark. "You wouldn't happen to be the same Arthur C. Doyle who went-on about fairies, would you... The one who published in *The Strand* about those... what were they called, Cottingley Fairies?"

Doyle felt his face flush, though he tried to keep his composure. "Yes, I did publish an account of the Cottingley Fairies, and I believed photographs documenting their existence were genuine."

Mulligan withheld a laugh and glanced at the younger constable standing beside him. The lad named Hewitt barely contained his amusement since Doyle started his story. "Well, I'll be. I would've loved to have seen your face when those fairies matched cutouts from a children's book."

"So, you're saying you want us to believe this poor fool MacLeod was driven to his death by fairies, do you?" observed Sergeant Mulligan taking back the conversation from his subordinate.

"Not fairies - spirits" said Doyle regretting the statement as soon as he said it.

"Spirits, now," sneered Hewitt.

Doyle paused and chose his words carefully. "MacLeod seemed to believe he was being pursued by something dark from a past encounter with a ship in the Arctic. I can't explain it in full without investigating further, but…"

Mulligan cut him off again, his joviality gone. "This sounds like another one of your spiritual shenanigans. Look, Dr. Doyle, this is a simple case of a drunken sailor losing his balance. We don't have time to chase shadows just because you've got a taste for selling stories. And this business about seances—well, I'd say it's not only a waste of police time but borders on the hysterical."

Hewitt nodded eagerly, eyes glinting with mirth as he chimed in. "You might be onto something with stories and mysteries in your books, mystery writer, but this is real life. Just a sad, drunk sailor who went a little too far up the mast."

Doyle felt a deep pang of frustration as he looked between the two men. Yet, he persisted, his voice measured. "Would you at least have someone assess the body for more than just alcohol? I believe there may have been substances involved. MacLeod was hallucinating, claiming he saw 'demons.' This isn't something that should be ignored. I can assist…I'm a physician after all."

Mulligan sighed with a note of exasperation. "Fine. I'll send Mr. Cross—the chemist. Our own doctor's gone out to attend an emergency a few villages over, so Cross will have to do." He spoke dismissively as he moved toward the gangplank to the dock. "But I don't want any more of this nonsense about spirits or 'ghost ships,' you hear me?"

Doyle nodded, biting back his retort. Their dismissive smirks stayed with him, a reminder of the lingering sting from the Cottingley Fairies incident. Hopefully the chemist, Mr. Cross, would be more reasonable.

Chapter
The Chemist

A short time later, chemist Alistair Cross arrived at the dock where the tragic scene unfolded less than an hour before. Mr. Cross was a wiry man with an alert, inquisitive expression. His wire-rimmed glasses glinted as he surveyed the scene, paying careful attention to every detail with the same meticulousness Doyle himself often used. "I was summoned by Detective Sergeant Mulligan. I must say I was excited to meet you, Dr. Doyle."

"And I you, Mr. Cross, sincerely so."

"I've read your works on Mr. Holmes—I find the deductive methods fascinating. I'll admit, I've tried my hand at employing them myself, in my little apothecary."

"Is that so?" Doyle responded with genuine interest. "I'm pleased to hear it. Deductive reasoning is invaluable in our medical profession - wouldn't you say?"

"Oh, certainly," Cross replied, his tone lively. "You'd be surprised at how many people come in convinced they know their ailment—sprains they believe are fractures, or a mild headache they insist is something fatal. Observation, subtle questioning—it helps me see beyond what they think they know to the underlying cause and medicinal treatment."

Doyle chuckled. "I do the same in my practice. My mentor, Dr. Bell, was the actual source of the deductive method. He was also a keen observer of human nature, able to deduce occupation, habits, and even recent travels of his patients with a mere glance. That's what makes it crucial for criminal investigations."

"I wish I could have seen him at his work," said Cross still crouching next to MacLeod's body.

MacLeod lay twisted and contorted, his limbs bent unnaturally as if he had fought gravity itself on his descent. His hands were scraped raw from gripping the mast rigging, and his face bore an expression of sheer terror, eyes still open, staring blankly into the distance.

"I was told he raved about demons?" commented Cross not looking up from MacLeod's scarred arms and hands. "For a sailor, such superstitious notions aren't uncommon, but with a fall like this..." He trailed off, tapping his chin thoughtfully.

Doyle nodded. "He was definitely under some kind of mental duress. He'd been muttering about apparitions from the *Octavius*, a derelict ship the crew encountered years ago. Doyle gave a quick explanation of the encounter, their reunion, seance and unsolved mystery of the death years earlier under similar circumstances. Doyle concluded saying, "MacLeod claimed they were 'coming for him'—it was as if he believed some supernatural force was present, hunting him down."

Cross nodded stepping aside for two men waiting to load the body on a stretcher. "It could be a case of paranoia exacerbated by alcohol or...other substances. Do you know if he had anything unusual to eat or drink before his death?"

"Not definitively," Doyle admitted. "Mulligan suggested it was merely a drunken accident, but I've seen enough to know when something's amiss."

Cross stood and pondered something for a moment, then seemed to come to a decision. "Since our local physician is not available, and you are frankly more qualified to conduct a medical examination, would you consider an autopsy, Doctor?"

"Do you think Sergeant Mulligan might object?" Doyle asked pensively. "He didn't think much of my thoughts - especially given some recent press on an investigation I conducted in Cottingley."

"Most of Mulligan's calls involve dealing with drunks at the pub, domestic arguments, and the like. So, I've no doubt he would ascribe this to just another drunkard. The victim wasn't a local and has no apparent connections to Mulligan's betters, so he won't give two hoots about what we do from here."

Doyle simply nodded. He was going to like this chemist.

Chapter
Another Autopsy

Doyle stood over the MacLeod's body after it was taken to what served as the local morgue. His hands were steady as he worked with surgical precision. Beside him, Cross observed silently, occasionally handing Doyle the instruments he requested.

MacLeod's body lay still, cold and pale beneath the lamplight. His face, though lifeless, still bore the faint traces of terror, lips slightly parted as if caught in a final, silent scream. Doyle had seen many deaths over the years, but the manner in which MacLeod had died felt personal.

"Doctor," Cross said quietly, breaking the heavy silence. "What do you see so far?"

Doyle paused for a moment, glancing down at MacLeod's motionless form. "Poison," he said simply, his voice carrying a note of certainty. "I've seen the signs before. The discoloration of the skin, the dilation of the pupil, the condition of the liver... it doesn't fit with anything natural."

Cross frowned, studying the body more closely. "What kind of poison?"

"That's the mystery, isn't it?" Doyle murmured as he bent lower, his fingers delicately tracing the outline of MacLeod's neck. "Given the unknown substances encountered on the *Octavius,* and myriad of things that can be obtained by a sailor, it could be anything."

"If I were to venture a guess as a chemist, based on the symptoms, we could be looking at something derived from an opiate or perhaps a derivative of datura. Both could cause hallucinations and delirium."

Doyle straightened, removing his blood-stained gloves, and placed them on the nearby table. "Opiates, yes. They are subtle things, mixed in food or drink, undetectable until it's too late. However, there are many pharmaceutical culprits to choose from."

Cross's looked closer at the mouth and eyes. "I can take what we need from here and do analysis at my shop. I've done some work for the constabulary in another town."

Doyle nodded. "Brilliant. We'll need the proof."

Without another word, Doyle set to work, carefully extracting a small tissue sample from MacLeod's liver and placing it into a glass vial. "This," he said, holding the little container up to the lamplight, "should get you started."

Cross took the vial from Doyle with a gentle but deliberate hand. "I'll run the necessary tests right away. I'll look for alkaloids —signs of plant-based toxins, opiates, or anything foreign. I can compare this to known substances and see what we're dealing with."

"And if you find something?" Doyle asked, his voice low.

Cross's lips pressed into a thin line. "If we find something, then we know for certain this wasn't the work of alcohol or some supernatural force. It's murder, plain and simple."

"We don't have much time," warned Doyle. "The rest of the crew has made it clear that they're leaving as soon as they get their £100. That could be within days."

"Understood."

Chapter
Doyle Nightmare

It was late when Doyle finally retired to his narrow bunk after a smoke, the creaking of the ship was barely audible over the sound of his own thoughts. Sleep came surprisingly slow, tugging at the edges of his mind like a slow, persistent tide. His body, exhausted from the days events finally gave in and began to drift away.

In the twilight of his consciousness, the air around him grew thick and heavy, the temperature dropping until his breath became visible in the cold. Doyle found himself back on the *Herald* two decades earlier, but the ship seemed... different. Its timbers groaned unnaturally as though the vessel itself were alive, breathing with the pulse of the sea. Fog, dense and ghostly, rolled across the deck, obscuring everything beyond a few feet.

He turned slowly and found MacLeod standing at the edge of the mist. The now dead crewman stared at him with glassy eyes, his face frozen in the same terror it had shown on the autopsy table. His mouth opened, as if to speak, but no sound came out.

"MacLeod," Doyle whispered, his voice trembling. "What... what happened to you?"

MacLeod took a step forward, his movements slow and jerky, like a marionette tugged on invisible strings. His lips moved again, forming words that Doyle couldn't hear. Doyle stumbled backward, his heart racing. His surroundings shifted unnaturally as the fog enveloped him. The planks beneath his feet became slippery, coated with a thin layer of ice. As he turned to flee, more figures appeared—silent, unmoving. They were the crew of the *Octavius*. The dead sailors stood in a ghostly line, their faces pale and frostbitten, eyes dull and lifeless. The captain was still clutching that cursed logbook while standing next to a coffin with the Chinese marking. Each crewman's expression held the same twisted mix of fear and resignation, as though they had been waiting for him all along. One of them, a gaunt figure with ice in his beard and hollow cheeks, raised a skeletal hand and pointed directly at Doyle.

"Only death comes from Thistle Mountain. " came a faint whisper, cold and hollow, echoing in the night air. "Your death..."

Panic surged through Doyle's veins. He tried to run but his boots slipped on the icy deck while the fog thickened around him like a suffocating shroud. The dead men followed silently, their footsteps nonexistent, but he could feel their presence, closer and closer with each passing second. The voices grew louder, filling his ears with incoherent whispers containing *Thistle Mountain, My King* and a new warning about *The Way*. Doyle's feet got some traction and he began to move away. He could still feel them close behind —too close—but he dared not look back. His legs ached, his heart thundered in his chest, but no matter how fast he ran, he couldn't escape the cold. Suddenly, the ship seemed to shift beneath him, its timbers cracking, splitting apart. Doyle lost his balance, pitching forward into the swirling fog, into the dark abyss that waited below. He fell into nothingness.

Doyle awoke with a violent jolt, his body trembling and slick with cold sweat. His eyes flew open, and the fog of his nightmare dissipated into the predawn gloom of the real world. But something wasn't right. He wasn't in his bunk anymore. He was outside—on the deck of the *Herald*.

The chill of the night air bit at his skin, and as he blinked in confusion, he realized he was standing perilously close to the edge

148

of the ship's railing. His heart raced, not from the nightmare, but from the sudden, stark realization that he was mere inches from plunging into the cold, black waters below.

"Doyle!" Banes called sharply.

He spun around, disoriented. Three of his old shipmates now approached, their faces pale with alarm. Baines rushed forward and grabbed Doyle, pulling him back from the edge.

"Are you mad? We thought... we thought you were about to kill yourself just like MacLoud."

Doyle's mind struggled to piece together what had just happened. He looked at Banes and then at Garret, Li and Winthrop, their eyes wide with fear.

"I... I don't know how I got here?" Doyle muttered, his throat dry and his body still shivering from the remnants of his dream. "I must've walked in my sleep. I had a nightmare about the *Octavius*."

"It's the curse…" said Banes.

"No," Doyle said, trying to steady his breath. His mind raced, still grasping at the vestiges of reason. "It's not... it's not just the derelict ship. There's something else going on here."

"Not you too Doyle,' exclaimed Garret.

"This is different," objected Doyle. "I was asleep. It was just a very vivid nightmare."

"Folk don't go wanderin' out in the cold, nor near leap off a ship to drown themselves, not from a mere nightmare," responded Garret.

Doyle said nothing, his thoughts swirling with doubt and confusion. He glanced over his shoulder, back toward the railing, as if half-expecting to see the ghostly figures of his dream lurking in the shadows.

149

"I'll meet back with the chemist, Cross, and Madame Seraphine. Either I was given some drug, or the spirits are trying to communicate. Either way, I'll get to the bottom of it."

"What could they try to communicate?" asked Baines. "Something about the killer…"

"It felt like more of a warning…something about *The Way.*"

"Ye mean the way through the Northwest Passage?" asked Garret

"I've no idea," said Doyle. "You know how dreams are. It was probably nothing."

Chapter
Chemist Update

It was late morning when Doyle and Seraphine made their way down the cobbled streets to Cross's apothecary. The building itself was modest but well-kept, a quaint structure of red brick with a curved glass window displaying rows of neat, apothecary bottles in green and deep blue. The sign above the door contained the name "Cross & Co. Chemist."

The shop felt both welcoming and clinical. Rows of shelves lined the walls, each packed with various tinctures, oils, herbs and powders, neatly labeled in Cross's precise handwriting. A counter stood at the back, partitioned off by glass cases containing rare medicinal items, an array of surgical tools, and jars filled with foreign ingredients in their raw form.

Cross welcomed them with a polite nod, leading them through a narrow door at the back of the shop into his lab—a compact but functional workspace. A large workbench dominated the center, littered with glass beakers, crucibles and other apparatus. A faint smell of sulfur and herbs lingered in the air, mingling with the acrid, unmistakable odor of something recently burned.

"I'm glad you're here, Doctor. I'm also pleased to meet you, Madame Seraphine. I've made some progress, though my examination isn't quite complete."

Seraphine cast her eyes around the room noting the jars filled with preserved specimens, roots, and various powders meticulously organized along one wall. "Your work here is fascinating, Mr. Cross. It feels as though each shelf holds its own wisdom."

"It certainly is a collection," he said, wiping his hands on a cloth. "I'm sure you'll agree that the field of medicine, after all, has always been balanced between scientific rigor and a certain… spiritual understanding."

Madame Seraphine smiled at the attempt to recognize her possible contribution.

"I've seen how belief can influence health—especially in cases of 'cures' driven by the mind alone," added Doyle. While not exactly corroborating Cross's point, it showed an openness to whatever they find.

Cross gave a thoughtful nod, pouring the last of a dark liquid from a beaker into a measuring vial. "Precisely. There's a recognition among many physicians today that the patient's belief, their spirit, if you will, can act as a catalyst in treatment. In this case, however, we have something more tangible."

Cross turned to a workbench where an arrangement of samples taken from MacLeod's liver lay carefully labeled. "I've run some initial tests. First, I tested for common toxins—opium, laudanum, belladonna, the usual culprits of choice by sailors."

"Did you find anything?" Seraphine asked.

"Yes and no," Cross said, adjusting his glasses. "What I found was neither simple opium nor alcohol but something more exotic—an alkaloid from the Orient I've yet to fully identify. However, it shares chemical properties with a rare compound derived from the seeds of the *Ephedra Sinica* plant."

Doyle raised an eyebrow. "Ephedra? Isn't that used in traditional Chinese medicine?"

"Indeed," Cross replied. "But in higher concentrations, it can have intense psychoactive effects including hallucinations and erratic behavior. What's puzzling is that this variant has been modified somehow. My theory is that it's been combined with another substance—possibly *Datura*, a nightshade."

Madame Seraphine's eyes widened. "You mean the eyedrops used by some women to dilate their eyes to look more seductive."

"That's correct," said Cross. "I believe the combination could increase heart rate, induce anxiety and trigger great paranoia."

"So, in MacLeod's case, it would explain his fear of 'demons' from the *Octavius*," concluded Seraphine.

"It's highly probable," Cross confirmed. "I'll need another day or so to be certain, but this mixture would be difficult to detect without specific knowledge of its components."

Doyle nodded thoughtfully. "Whoever did this would need more than just a passing knowledge of drugs, or have access to some bad characters to supply it."

Cross and Madame Seraphine exchanged a tense glance. The murderer could be part of a very dangerous group.

"Do you think the quantity could be limited precisely enough to more control its effects. In my case, could it have caused an extreme nightmare ending in sleepwalking - but not uncontrolled hysteria like MacLeod?" Doyle paused to explain his terror the previous night that ended in standing precariously at a frozen precipice.

Cross thought for a moment. "If the person had enough knowledge to combine these agents together, I suppose they could control its administration to that degree."

"Why would they do that?" asked Seraphine. "Isn't it more likely that they just gave an insufficient dose. Doyle may not have consumed enough of the poison to be killed, like MacLeod."

"Unless they didn't want to murder the good doctor," countered Cross. "They knew he was getting close and did it as a warning."

After a pause, Doyle seemed to have new determination. "What's the next step in your experiments?"

"I believe I have the correct combination. However, I don't know how it was delivered. I assume it was contained in some food, drink or tobacco. But each of those items could alter it's effectiveness."

"Perfect, Mr. Cross. If we have a better idea of the source, we can determine how it was done - slight of hand or something else," commented Seraphine.

"If it was done with theatrical tricks, that's where *your* expertise comes in," confirmed Doyle.

Chapter
The Seminary

With Cross finishing his experiments, Doyle and Seraphine decided to pursue the possibility that that Thistle Mountain and the cargo symbol may represent a Christian sect. They hired a carriage and arrived at Stonehill Seminary where Father Elijah Grantham welcomed them into his book-laden office. Dusty volumes and old scrolls lined the walls, stacked in every available space, filling the room with an air of ancient scholarship. Grantham gestured for them to sit.

"We're interested in this symbol," said Doyle pushing across a drawing. "It might be linked to a place called Thistle Mountain."

"So, you want information on the Taiping Rebellion..." Grantham said casually.

Doyle looked shocked by the ready answer.

"Are they so commonly known?" asked Seraphine.

"I wouldn't say they're commonly known by most people in the West. Unless that person was linked to Opium Wars in the Orient"

"How so?" asked Doyle.

Grantham adjusted his spectacles thoughtfully. "There was once a disturbing figure named Hong Xiuquan. His story began during a bout of fever where he experienced what he believed was a divine vision. Hong claimed to have traveled to a heavenly land in the East where his 'Father' told him that demons were corrupting humanity. In his vision, Hong fought these demons with the aid of his 'brother.'"

"His brother?" asked Doyle.

Grantham leaned forward, emphasizing his next words. "He believed his brother was none other than Jesus Christ. He began calling himself the *Heavenly King*, and declared his divine purpose to fight demonic forces in China."

"King?" Doyle interjected looking at Seraphine. "Would a follower refer to Hong as *My King*..."

"That's possible," Grantham affirmed. "Hong was convinced that he alone had the right to save China, under his title *Heavenly King* and *Lord of the Kingly Way*. At first, he was seen as a madman, but his resolve only grew. In time, he gathered followers, many of them from a marginalized group called the Hakka. He set up a stronghold on Thistle Mountain in 1847, a place steeped in local mystique and symbolism. This location became the birthplace of his uprising and the heart of the military force he assembled."

"Thistle Mountain," Doyle echoed. "We found that place mentioned along with a reference to My King."

"Thistle Mountain itself was remote, and the Hakka worshippers indeed held it sacred. You can partly see why they embraced the man claiming to be the Heavenly King on that spot. Soon, Hong commanded his followers not only spiritually but militarily. The movement readily expanded. By 1851, he'd proclaimed the beginning of the '*Taiping Heavenly Kingdom*' and called his people to war."

"Remarkable," Doyle exclaimed, imagining the fiery passion of Hong's followers. "He assembled an entire army for war - not your typical cult leader."

"No. He was partly helped by circumstance. China was struggling with mass opium addition supplied by the West which the Emperor's administration was unable to stop. " Grantham said, his face grave. "Hong seized on the hatred of opium and vowed to make it stop.   From Thistle Mountain, they waged war across China, spreading their beliefs by the sword. They took the city of Nanjing in 1853, turning it into the capital of their *Heavenly Kingdom*. There, Hong's control grew. He outlawed vices in addition to the use of opium. Hong enforced separation between men and women, and maintained strict religious codes of his own creation. His followers lived in constant fear of corporal punishment."

"So, he turned into a tyrant," Seraphine said cooly.

"Indeed," Grantham replied, his expression somber. "But it gets worse. The Taiping Rebellion...as it became known, claimed the lives of seventy million people. We know it as the Second Opium War after the United States and England became embroiled in the conflict to protect Christian missionaries and trade."

Seraphine gasped, pressing a hand to her mouth. "Seventy million? That's almost the population of Europe."

Grantham nodded grimly. "Consider this: more people died in the Taiping Rebellion than three times the population of the entire United States of America. We're talking about a level of devastation that is, frankly, unfathomable. Every man, woman and child killed when the emperor decided to eliminate this *virus*.   It was a catastrophe of unprecedented scale, one caused by a man who claimed to be the Son of God, no less."

Doyle furrowed his brow. "It's almost a foreshadowing of the devastation described in Revelation."

"Quite literally," Grantham said, his tone sharp with disapproval. "Hong proclaimed that the visions had shown him the 'Father' and his 'brother'—Jesus himself. Imagine that! A blasphemous claim if ever there was one. When he told his

157

followers he was Christ's brother and a king, they believed him. His followers accepted his authority as divinely sanctioned, as if his word alone could move the world. Nothing good can come from listening to any man who claims to be divinely linked to Christ. Or, somebody claiming to access spirits in another realm."

Seraphine shifted uncomfortably. "But, Father, how could so many become believers that quickly. Could it be that he had good motives, at least in the beginning?"

Grantham sighed. "Perhaps in the beginning. Hong's followers were largely the oppressed, the downtrodden, the dispossessed. The promise of a better life, of shared wealth and heavenly reward... that can be a powerful lure. But it plunged a nation into a horrific bloodbath. Half truths are equally, or even more dangerous, than lies."

"What happened to this, Hong?" asked Seraphine.

"We was said to have died by his own hand. A terrible fate for a terrible man," said Grantham shaking his head.

"Looking to our situation," said Doyle. "Why would a ship in the Arctic have references to *Thistle Mountain* and *My King* a decade later? The movement was long gone."

"I don't understand..." said Grantham.

Doyle and Seraphine explained their current mystery and its link to the *Octavius* with these references in the ship's log. They ended with, "Could it drive the captain to find the Northwest Passage when others more qualified had made the attempt ending in their deaths?"

"Absolutely," answered Grantham. "People believing they are involved in a divine quest, no matter how misguided, will do such things. The fact that simple farmers and peasants took on the

the Chinese Imperial Army is evidence of that. The question is *why?*"

"You mean why would the *Octavius* be linked to the cult and why would anything be gained by retrieving it?" clarified Seraphine.

"Precisely," affirmed Grantham. Just then a bell rang somewhere in the seminary and Grantham stood. "I regret that I'm late for vespers. Besides, I must research these perplexing questions more. I have a strange idea and need to consult with another librarian, formerly in the Alps."

Grantham walked Doyle and Seraphine to the entrance. As them exited the large front doors, Doyle commented to Seraphine, "You know the dream I mentioned...the dead crew seemed to warn me about *The Way.*

"Grantham mentioned *The Kingly Way* and *The Heavily Way*. Is *The Way* a simple abbreviation?" asked Seraphine.

"I don't know... Why a warning about a dead cult, and why not use it's exact name?"

"While we're at it," interjected Seraphine scanning for a cab for hire with none in sight. "What could possibly involve the Alps?"

Chapter
The Man from the Alps

They arrived again at Eleanor's bookstore on their way back from the seminary. While they recapped their findings at the seminary and inquired what Eleanor's contacts at other groves yielded.

"I think I've found some chatter you'll find intriguing. Oddly enough, there's been talk—quiet, mind you—about a man of Swiss descent who's been approaching the local groves and druidic circles, asking if they'd like to join a movement he calls 'The Way.'"

"Swiss, really..." exclaimed Doyle.

"Yes, definitely Swiss...though he dressed and talked like a banker. I thought it was unrelated until your visit to the seminary. Now it seems strikingly similar to the Chinese group you described —without any direct mention of 'Heaven' or 'King.' Just... *The Way.* Odd coincidence given his arrival at the same time as your *Herald* reunion wouldn't you say?"

Doyle raised an eyebrow, glancing at Seraphine. "Strange indeed."

"Let's think this through beginning with why approach the groves..." said Seraphine. "It sounds like this man is being strategic, possibly even clever, in how he presents his movement - 'The Way'- it almost sounds appealing, or at least, innocuous."

Eleanor's brows knit together. "Dropping any reference to 'Heaven' or a 'King' might be a calculated move to attract the followers of Druidism. As you know, Druid beliefs center on a deep reverence for nature - emphasizing harmony with the earth and its cycles. Groves seek wisdom through communion with the natural world, not the 'establishment'."

"You mean, the groves avoid anything having to do with government and organized religion. So, any reference to heaven or king would drive them away," interjected Seraphine,

"Exactly. By framing it as 'The Way,' he taps into the same reverence for balance and harmony that many of these groups already hold dear. And for people who are drawn to the earth and to spiritual practices like those in the local groves, it could be a natural fit."

Eleanor stopped to retrieve a small notebook from beneath the counter and flipped it to a marked page. "When I asked a few of my contacts, they said he's been careful in his approach, speaking of restoring the 'balance' and helping humanity return to an older, purer path. They said he even displayed a symbol that looked Chinese, but it didn't exactly match what you described."

"Maybe they have a different symbol now..." mused Doyle.

"I assume so," responded Eleanor. "If they're altering the name to attract druids and possibly others, they may have altered the symbol too. That might be a link to the *Herald* or their misfortunes."

"I don't see how this group could be involved in the death of Silas for sure. Its also seems unlikely that they could somehow get access to the *Herald* and slip some drug to MacLeod and even Doyle for that matter," said Seraphine to Doyle.

"I agree. If there's some link, I don't see it exactly Let's pause and look at the obvious difference. Now it appears that a *Swiss businessman,* not a *Chinese holy man,* seems to be recruiting people to form a new group that's *slightly* similar to a dead cult across the world. How could that be?"

Seraphine mused. 'On the other hand, he is here in a remote part of England at *exactly* the same time as the *Herald* reunion…"

The three stood in silence contemplating the new mystery. Things were becoming complicated.

"Let's focus on what we do know," said Eleanor. "He's approaching the local groves with what appears to be a warped version of your *Heavenly Way*. Since a man like him is unlikely to be a friend of our spiritual circle, or the Heavenly Way, he must have another goal. Given his appearance at this time and place, it must involve the *Herald*."

Doyle nodded in agreement. "If this Swiss man's purpose were purely spiritual, he'd follow the original teachings without alteration. The fact that he's molding them to appeal to an entirely different culture suggests an ulterior motive. What is it?"

Eleanor bit her lip. "One of my contacts mentioned that he spoke about 'resetting the world to set things right.'"

"To do that, he'd have to attract *lots* of followers. Is he having any success?"

"Not that I've heard. There's nothing particularly spiritual about this man; he doesn't carry himself like a sage or a seeker. So, he's being shunned. I assume he'll target others outside the spiritual circle."

There was a brief, heavy silence as they stood dumbfounded. After some additional discussion, they concluded with Eleanor promising to pass along anything news that came her way.

Chapter
Li Second Interview

As Doyle and Seraphine left the bookstore, the damp chill of the northern air seemed to bite deeper than before. The conversation with Eleanor and the theologian had drawn connections that stretched all the way back to China, possibly elsewhere. They exchanged thoughtful glances as they walked toward the *Herald*, the implications weighing on them both.

"It seems to always lead back to the Far East," Seraphine declared as they crossed a cobbled street. "If these men — or this pagan group, or whatever it is — are operating in secret, there's little chance this *Octavius* was just another cargo ship."

"There was obviously something strange about the cargo," said Doyle thinking back. "Just the recurrence of the strange symbol is partial proof of that."

"Li said it was nonsensical," added Seraphine. "What did it look like again?"

"The drawing shows a circle above some other strange symbol. I was starting to assume it was some sort of company stamp from the shipper - perhaps not," said Doyle.

"We need to talk to Mr. Li. He was apparently able to read it. That's the only way he could declare it nonsensical," said Seraphine increasing her walk to the *Herald*.

They reached the *Herald* and made their way to the galley where Li would be. The scent of salted fish and herbs greeted them as they entered. Li looked up, a flicker of surprise in his dark eyes, but he nodded respectfully.

"Dr. Doyle, Madame," he greeted by bowing slightly.

Doyle approached him with a polite nod. "Li, there's something we wanted to ask you — it's about the symbol on the cargo crates of the *Octavius.*"

Li stopped his work as if being approached by something of grave concern.

"I said before….made no sense."

"However, you did confirm that it had Chinese elements. Can you explain how it can be Chinese, but make no sense?"

Li's gaze shifted downward, and he exhaled slowly. "Chinese writing...it not like English. Each character, it show a thought, a meaning. Like picture. Symbols are added together to make little picture - not like English letters make a word; Chinese symbols reveal idea. Not so simple."

Doyle nodded, sensing that Li was searching for the right words. "And the picture made of different symbols are put together to form an idea…its the *idea* on the cargo that made no sense…"

Li nodded. "That idea made no sense. One part is the symbol of many gods. Usually, it looks like temple roof, with many lines and marks for gods inside. But over it, there was another symbol — a circle, like halo, as you say."

"What does a halo mean?" asked Seraphine.

"The halo...it strange addition. Usually, halo mean one god, or new god. Sometimes, it mean Christian God," Li explained, his voice lowering as he glanced around cautiously. "But when circle placed over symbol of traditional gods, it does not make sense. It is conflict. Old ways do not meet new ways."

Doyle frowned. "Have you ever seen that combination before?"

"No!" said Li with agitation.

Doyle and Seraphine exchanged glances as if waiting for elaboration. None came.

After a couple more questions with little result, they thanked Li and made their way on deck.

"Do you believe him about not seeing it before?" asked Seraphine.

"No," replied Doyle.

Chapter
News of Winthrop

Doyle and Seraphine retreated back to the inn where they sat across from each other in a quiet corner. Clinking cups and mugs filling the space. They mulled over the tangled web of clues they'd gathered. The fire crackled nearby, but its warmth did little to ease the chill of uncertainty between them.

Seraphine took a thoughtful sip of tea, setting her cup down with a frown. "We have a complicated set of suspects and new elements. Its truly confusing."

Doyle nodded. "Let's lay it all out, we'll layer our new information over what we got from each crewman."

Seraphine nodded in agreement.

"Firstly, MacLeod was a loud, superstitious bully. He could have been on the wrong side of everyone through his role as chief boatswain. MacLeod could have observed something that got him killed. Let's assume anybody had motive and opportunity for his death…"

"Agreed," said Seraphine. "We'll keep things simple and take his death out of the equation. No sense in trying to layer something over it yet."

Doyle paused as a group passed the table. Talk of murder could draw a crowd they didn't need. He took a drink and waited. After a moment, Doyle continued, "Baines spent years in the Orient as a sailmaker - plenty of time to pick up knowledge of the local drugs or to fall in with... questionable groups. But would he really have gone so far as to join a Chinese cult?"

Seraphine shook her head. "It's too far-fetched, but Baines *did* seem to have a small grudge with Silas. If he was involved in any sort of opium trade, it would explain how he could access something strong enough to cause hallucinations, and death."

Doyle looked down at his tea, stirring it absently. "Then there's Moore, the storekeeper. He went through the *Octavius* cargo during the search and certainly would have had the opportunity to keep some of the more... potent substances. Silas *had* accused him of skimming off the top in the past."

"But he showed signs of being drugged himself," Seraphine pointed out, her fingers tracing the edge of her saucer thoughtfully. "Just like Silas."

"True," Doyle conceded. "That does complicate things. If he was a victim, we might be chasing the wrong lead. But it doesn't erase the fact that Moore had both opportunity, motive and a possible link to some Chinese supplier that could be linked to a cult."

Seraphine sighed, rubbing her temple. "Then there's Winthrop, the owner's son. He's a dubious character by all accounts—a gambler known to have squandered the family fortune. His conflicts with Silas seem to have been longstanding. But could he have brought an opium derivative onboard?"

Doyle raised an eyebrow. "Possibly, if he'd been exposed to it in his youth. Wealthy men's sons in certain social circles sometimes find themselves mingling with all manner of pricey vices."

"Winthrop's motivations are murky, I'll grant you..." Seraphine responded. "But, he may not be clever enough to orchestrate all this. Plus, a link to a cult seems unlikely. However, if there was money to be made, than anything's possible..."

Doyle leaned forward. "And then there's Li. He was unaccounted for on the *Octavius* when we were gathering to leave. We also can't ignore his extensive knowledge of Chinese herbs."

"He might have access to the kinds of toxins we're dealing with," agreed Seraphine. "When we questioned him about that cargo symbol, he seemed too quick to say he'd never seen it before. He could be hiding some link to a Chinese cult."

Doyle's looked conflicted as he considered Li. "I have difficulty with the thought of Li as a killer. Despite having some small conflict with Silas and the crew over cooking, I always took Li to be an upright man. I'll grant that here's some mystery surrounding him, but I really don't see him as a murderer."

They sat in silence for a moment, both lost in thought as they stared into the depths of their tea. Then, Seraphine's eyes widened slightly. "What about Captain Garret. He's a bit of a mystery. You know so little about him despite having spent so much time together."

Doyle nodded slowly, his brows furrowing. "However, he's been a steady captain, pragmatic, even... and why would he harm Silas? A harpooner of Silas's skill would only be an asset to him. Would he have a motive we're not seeing yet?"

"Perhaps something beyond his role as captain?" Seraphine suggested. "He could have an agenda none of us know about. That could be a tie to the strange Swiss businessman..."

After another pause, Doyle attempted to succinctly put it all together. "Each of them had access to Silas and MacLeod. Any one of them could have poisoned him, directly or indirectly, and finished the job with a marlinspike. I'm beginning to wonder if we're looking at one person, or if more than one man is hiding something."

171

Seraphine looked annoyed at the thought "It was hard enough to solve with one killer. The thought of two, or even more, makes my head throb."

"Forget I mentioned it," said Doyle with an equal lack of enthusiasm.

The innkeeper came to the parlor and quietly summoned them. "There's been an incident at the harbor. The constabulary requests your presence. It has something to do with a man named Winthrop."

Doyle and Seraphine gathered their coats and hurried through the cobblestone streets. They emerged onto the main thoroughfare where a crowd had gathered on the road near the docks. Lying before them was a half-covered figure under a rough blanket. Sergeant Mulligan was standing next to it writing in a notebook.

Doyle approached glancing sidelong at the contorted form under the covering. Seraphine looked pale as she took in the scene looking more vulnerable than before.

Mulligan turned to Doyle with a faint smirk. "Ah, Dr. Doyle. I hear you've continued playing detective with the chemist. Waste of time, if you ask me. But since this death seems similar to the last, I didn't want to be accused of not playing nice with the public."

Doyle ignored the jab and approached the body. "How did it happen?"

Mulligan turned back a page in his notebook and read his entry. "The deceased, by the name of Carter Winthrop, stumbled off the *Herald* like the devil was chasing him. Made it halfway across the street when a carriage rounded the bend at full speed.

172

The carriage driver reported that Winthrop appeared wild drunk...
horses trampled him." With that, Mulligan closed his notebook
with a clap as if concluding the whole affair.

Seraphine winced and glanced at Mulligan. "Is Captain
Garret aware?"

Sergeant Mulligan rolled his eyes. "Already interviewed
him. Said Winthrop had a taste for drink and a gambler's luck,
which is to say none at all. Just another drunken incident is my
take."

Doyle stepped closer, casting a keen eye over Winthrop's
body beneath the blanket. "You seem awfully certain," he
remarked coolly.

The sergeant straightened, crossing his arms. "Listen, I
know the type. Nothing more than an accident. This place doesn't
need a crime writer conjuring up some grand conspiracy." His lips
curled with a smirk. "Or trying to play detective with the chemist."

Doyle bristled but held his composure. "I'd like to examine
him. Just a brief look if I may?"

"Examine him?" Barked Mulligan with a laugh. "I've
already indulged you too much."

Doyle stood silent staring at Mulligan as a silent challenge.

"All right, then. Take two minutes and be off with you. The
mortician's wagon is here."

Kneeling beside the body, Doyle gently lifted the edge of
the blanket, revealing Winthrop's face—pale, bruised, with eyes
closed in death. He scanned the exposed skin, looking for anything
unusual and found discoloring similar to Silas and MacLeod before
him. Doyle clipped a small sample of hair without notice. In a
single motion, he put the clipping in his pocket while pretending to
adjust his coat. "Thank you, Detective Sergeant."

173

Mulligan merely grunted. "Well, hope you're satisfied. This'll be just another sorry tale for that ship on its way to be scrapped."

"Her name is *Herald,* sir," retorted Doyle holding his anger.

Mulligan just shrugged and walked toward the mortician's wagon.

Doyle turned to Seraphine, his voice low. "We need to see what the Mr. Cross can make of the hair sample." He cast a final look at Winthrop's still form, the discolored skin nagging at his thoughts.

Sergeant Mulligan clapped his hands, signaling to the waiting mortuary assistants. "Take him to the cemetery."

Chapter
Seraphine Reveals a Secret

As they retreated along the cobblestone streets, Seraphine clutched Doyle's arm, her face white as a ghost.

"Are you okay?" asked Doyle.

She whispered, voice trembling. "Please, take me back to the inn."

Doyle was stunned, but complied and led her down the streets toward the warmth of the little hotel. He gestured toward the parlor that they'd just left and she nodded. Once seated, Doyle ordered tea and searched her face for understanding. Seraphine remained silent, gripping her bag tightly, as if debating what she was about to share. Finally, with a deep breath, she reached into her bag and pulled out a worn, ivory-colored whale tooth. Carved onto its surface were delicate, almost haunting engravings of children, their expressions of innocence somehow preserved in the faded lines.

Doyle's eyes widened. "That... that's Silas' scrimshaw. How did you get it?"

Seraphine swallowed hard, her voice barely above a whisper. "Silas was my brother."

For a moment, Doyle sat in silence. He opened his mouth to speak, but words failed him.

Seraphine looked down at the carving and caressed its edges in a way that indicated this was hardly the first time."I received it years ago. Captain Garret mailed it and his other things to my mother after Silas died. I kept it as a connection to my twin."

Doyle leaned forward, his voice softened. "Is that how you conjured him?"

175

She shook her head while sorrow permeated her face. "Not exactly. After we learned of Silas death, I kept track of the *Herald*. I followed its voyages, knowing it would eventually be retired. I needed to know what happened to Silas. When I found out it was to be scrapped after one final voyage, I had to create a plan to get onboard and determine what happened."

"What sort of plan?"

"It came to me while I was working in Bristol," she said naming the city where theaters dotted the streets. "I was an actress in its small theater district. When I took on the part of a medium in a play, it struck me to use my role to somehow get a seance on the *Herald*. I didn't know how it would help to find the killer exactly, but that would be my way in. The rest of the plan took time."

Doyle nodded indicating that he followed her reasoning so far.

"I made my way to London and gained similar roles leading to a reputation as a spiritualist. Then, out of nowhere, I received an invitation—a mysterious benefactor offering me a chance to host a seance on the *Herald*. I thought it was fate, perhaps even divine intervention."

She looked down at the whale tooth, still caressing it. "I used a photo of Silas to create his appearance at the seance through tricks of the trade. Its amazing what a candle, photographic plate and sleight of hand can create."

Doyle watched her closely, understanding the intricate planning and emotional toll this journey must have cost her. But he saw something else—fear, uncertainty. She obviously didn't expect the deaths that followed.

"This wasn't supposed to happen," she continued, voice cracking. "It was all supposed to end with one seance. I thought the killer would think it real and reveal himself. I didn't expect anyone to die. Now there's a second death and possibly more to come. It has to stop."

"Who helped you?"

"Nobody. On the stage its easy to employ an accomplice backstage. But on the *Herald* it would have been impossible to bring somebody aboard without being caught. So, I was limited to the use of photographic plates and a carefully placed candle to conjure ghosts. It was surprisingly easy in such a small space. A single candle had sufficient light to project the ghostly figure through the translucent glass plate onto a wall just feet away."

Doyle was stunned. "But how did you keep the glass plate concealed?"

"All were entranced before I even started due to their previous experiences from the *Octavius*. People saw what they expected to see and never looked past my gloved hands."

"Myself included," Doyle admitted.

Seraphine grabbed Doyle's hand with a fierce plea in her eyes. "I don't want more blood on my hands. I want to leave this place."

Doyle squeezed back. "I know this has gone farther than you ever intended. But now that we're here, we must see it through. If you leave now, we might never uncover who killed Silas, or why. Plus, it seems we may need to act before more people die. Stay, just a couple more days. I will be with you at all times and it will be my fault of anybody else dies."

She hesitated, the pain and weariness etched deeply into her face. After a long silence she gave a slight nod. "For Silas…"

178

Chapter
Chemist Conclusions

Doyle and Seraphine made their way through the narrow, winding streets to the chemist's apothecary. Inside, the familiar scent of sulfur, herbs, and chemicals filled the air. As they entered, Cross nodding in greeting.

"Dr. Doyle, Madame Seraphine. I've been expecting you. You'll be pleased to know that I've finally managed to identify how the poison was delivered." Cross set a vial down with a grave face. "To begin with, the substance is fast-acting but unstable. It doesn't retain potency for very long."

"So, it couldn't have come from the *Octavius*," Seraphine murmured.

"Correct," Cross nodded. "This poison couldn't have remained potent aboard a ship stranded in the ice, or the years that followed. It had to have been created recently."

"What about Silas two decades ago. Could one of the Herald's crew have brought a similar batch from the *Octavius* to kill him?" asked Doyle.

"Yes. It could last the length of a voyage. In fact, given how I think it was administered, the same type of drug is likely to have killed Silas too."

"How was it administered?" asked Seraphine excitedly. She was finally making progress on Silas' death.

"Based on the residue, I'd venture to say it was delivered through something smoked, like tobacco. The signs of numbness and confusion, followed by death is consistent with a calculated dosage in inhaled form."

"Tobacco would be an efficient method of delivery. Everyone smoked aboard the *Herald,*" remarked Doyle. "And still do…"

Seraphine swallowed, clutching Doyle's arm. "Is there any way to trace the source?"

Cross shook his head slowly. "Not directly, no. Its difficult to obtain outside specialized apothecaries or connections in certain circles - some with Oriental roots."

"The only person on the *Herald* with extensive knowledge of Chinese herbs and obvious links to the Orient is Li. We need to examine his pantry herbs and personal possessions. It won't be easy, so we'll need a plan *and* your skills of deception," said Doyle to Seraphine.

"There's no time like the present…," she replied.

Chapter
Li's Belongings

They stopped at a fine tobacco shop on route and gave each crewman a pouch as a gift. If the killer planned to kill again, they would need to find another means of distribution. The premium tobacco would keep each man supplied for at least a week, thwarting the killer's plans, at least temporarily.

The two split up after arriving on the *Herald*. Seraphine went to Li's location in the galley kitchen. His face was impassive - slicing vegetables with quiet efficiency. She took a moment to observe him, rehearsing her excuse before stepping forward.

"Mr. Li. Could you help me with something on deck? I noticed some trouble with the rigging that could pose a danger. I'd feel much better if you could take a look."

"I no sailor, Madame," said Li continuing to chop.

"Everyone else is somewhere enjoying their tobacco. You sure you can't help me?" she asked with her best damsel in distress look.

Li paused mid-slice, looking up at her. He seemed to assess her briefly, his dark eyes unreadable.

There was a flicker of something in his expression—mistrust or perhaps curiosity—but he wiped his hands. After one last glance around the kitchen, he followed her up the narrow staircase to the main deck.

As soon as they were clear, Doyle stepped out from his spot behind the bulkhead and slipped into the kitchen. The small space felt confined, thick with the smells of herbs, and whatever Li had been cooking. His eyes swept over the cluttered shelves lined with a few glass jars and meticulously stacked tins. Each jar held dried herbs, some labeled in neat, faded ink with Chinese characters. Doyle bent closer to examine each, but couldn't read the script to identify any contents. He carefully lifted a jar of dried leaves and held it up to the light, inspecting the faint scent it emitted — sharp and unfamiliar. None had the cult's character on any label. He realized the futility of examine the herbs - especially when Li would be unlikely to leave evidence of poison in the open. So he moved toward the far corner where a curtain shielded Li's personal bunk. Doyle parted the fabric to reveal a neat, almost sparse sleeping space. He glanced over his shoulder to ensure he was still alone, then began searching.

In Li's trunk, Doyle found miscellaneous clothing and a weathered Bible, the leather cover creased and softened from years of use. Doyle puzzled over Li having a bible when he never gave any inclination of being Christian. Doyle thumbed through the pages, pausing as a small photographic plate slipped out and landed on the bed. He picked it up, studying the faces in the worn image. It showed Li wearing a naval uniform while standing beside a woman with a soft, kind expression, and two young children. The uniform was adorned with markings that Doyle assumed belonged to the Chinese Imperial Navy. The little family looked happy, far removed from the hard-bitten cook Doyle had come to know. He wondered what had driven Li to leave a life as a naval officer with a contented family to cook in the belly of a whaling ship. Whatever the reason, Li lied about his past. The uniform is not something worn while working on Chinese river junks.

On deck, Seraphine led Li over to the rigging she'd mentioned, her demeanor relaxed, though her mind was racing with thoughts of Doyle below. She gestured toward a slightly disheveled coil of rope, doing her best to sound concerned. "Is this safe?"

Li looked perplexed as he stood over the line that seemed slightly altered as if kicked.

"It Safe," he said turning to go below.

"It looks terrifying to me," Seraphine said, hooking her arm through his, keeping her tone light as she worked to delay him. "Can we check the others?"

Li grunted, still studying her, as though deciding whether she was genuinely stupid, or simply stalling. After a moment, he walked the deck around the mainmast and glanced at the lines coiled on the deck or hanging from billy pins. He then nodded and abruptly scurried below.

Seraphine chased after him calling, "Mr. Li...Mr. Li..."

Li was too far ahead to be stopped and stepped into the galley. There he found Doyle casually sitting at a table. Doyle saw Li's expression shift, suspicion flickering across his face. He seemed to assess Doyle for a moment, his face now unreadable.

"Everything good up there?" Doyle asked, feigning ignorance.

Li nodded, then shifted his gaze to the shelf. "You here long time?"

"No," Doyle replied. "I saw you on deck with Madame Seraphine and decided to wait here for a cup of tea on your return."

Seraphine joined them, a slight smile on her face as she caught Doyle's eye. She managed to hide her relief, keeping her voice calm as she addressed Li. "Thanks for checking, Mr. Li. A cup of tea sounds lovely."

They made a production of casual small talk until they finished their tea and went topside. There, Doyle summarized his findings and the contents of the picture.

"The bible and naval officer's uniform might explain how the *Herald* came upon the *Octavius*. If Li was part of the quasi-christian cult and was familiar with the sea, he may have joined a whaler known to fish those waters in search for the ship," said Seraphine.

"I don't think so," continued Doyle. "The *Octavius* was lost on the other side of the North West Passage. Any professional mariner would know the impossibility of it surviving that frozen route. Even if they thought it possible to traverse when more capable vessels failed, the vast expanse of ocean fished by the whalers would make it a needle in a haystack."

"I suppose you're right. We're still missing part of the story."

"True," agreed Doyle. "Mr. Li is more of an enigma than ever."

Chapter
The Banking Alliance

Doyle and Seraphine decided to revisit Grantham at the seminary. They hoped his research with another librarian might yield the answer to the question: *What could be gained by retrieval of the Octavius?*

They arrived at the grand stone entrance of the seminary in the early afternoon. As they were guided back, they were greeted again with the scent of old leather-bound books and aged wood in the library. Grantham was waiting with a furrowed brow on a previously calm face. After a brief exchange of greetings, Grantham motioned for them to sit, while he retook his position behind the desk.

"Before I report my findings, please bring me up to date on your investigation."

Doyle leaned forward, folding his hands. "Particular to your findings, we've learned that a Swiss banker has been attempting to recruit followers from local Druidic groves for something called the 'The Way.' It sounds remarkably similar to the defunct cult we've been investigating, but it's been rebranded —stripped of references to *heaven* or a *king*."

Grantham raised an eyebrow. "A banker, you say? Not normally the type you'd expect to find on a spiritual quest. But it reinforces a finding regarding a possible reason to retrieve the *Octavius* and who might be behind it."

"We're all ears, Father. We haven't a clue how a Swiss businessman could be the key to our mystery," admitted Doyle.

Grantham looked troubled as began his narrative. "My research began with a different question. Specifically, *who* would have the resources to retrieve the *Octavius* cargo. The answer to that question led to the second."

"Beyond some government, I assume a banker or wealthy businessman would be the answer to the first question," conjectured Seraphine.

"Correct. In this case, it seems to be both in the form of a group called the Banking Alliance. To understand the group and their motives, we have to step back in history. The group's roots can be traced back to the early days of European banking families about two centuries ago. The rise of private banking institutions, notably in Switzerland, laid the foundation for unprecedented financial influence. These families understood that true power didn't lie in politics, but the money that supports them. In other words, kings and parliaments are controlled by those holding their debt."

"You mean, the bankers that lend them money," said Doyle.

"Correct," replied Grantham.

"I thought governments were financed through taxation?" commented Seraphine.

"You're getting to the crux of that matter," said Grantham with a smile. "If there is no debt, the bankers have no opportunity for profit. A need must be created for borrowing beyond what governments receive in taxes. What generates more government expenses and borrowing than any other event?"

"War, I suppose," said Seraphine.

"Correct again. One of this groups earliest successes was their manipulation of the Napoleonic Wars. By funding all sides of the conflict, Britain, France, Germany and France, they ensured a profit no matter the outcome. After these costly wars, the

186

economies of participating countries were shattered, which turned into more loans from these international bankers."

"That's absolutely insidious," said an incredulous Doyle.

"It gets worse...they were said to be involved with financing the American Civil War. More importantly for us, they were involved in the orchestrating the Opium Wars."

"What do you mean by 'orchestrating'," asked Doyle.

"Their involvement began after British merchants approaching China to buy European goods were rebuffed. The Chinese government basically said they had no need of anything Europe produced. The Banking Alliance helped their clients by finding a way to circumvent the imperial government and create a need for something Europe could acquire. Specifically, the Banking Alliance created a back door by having the merchants push opium acquired in India onto Chinese youth in exchange for silver, silk and other goods needed by these same merchants. The result was widespread addiction. Back home, people simply knew it as International Commerce, not knowing the real commodity. The Qing dynasty begged for relief stated that an entire generation was being wiped-out. They were even reputed to have mailed a personal plea to Queen Victoria herself."

"What was her reaction?" asked Seraphine.

"Its believed that the letter was intercepted and she never received it. Instead, Britain launched a military campaign to protect 'international commerce,' and keep the drugs flowing," said Grantham with obvious disgust.

"The financiers not only profited from the opium," Seraphine gasped, "but also from the war itself, through arms sales."

"Monstrous," Doyle muttered.

"You're probably wondering how this leads to the *Herald* and *Octavius*," said Grantham.

"I can see some vague connection, but please elaborate," said Doyle.

"As we previously discussed, the second Opium War coincided with the uprising by Hong Xiuquan and the Taiping Heavenly Way on Thistle Mountain. The Heavenly Way was against the use of Opium. His movement saw the Emperor as weak for failing to stop the growing Chinese addiction. I can only assume that the Banking Alliance ingratiated themselves with Hong and even contributed to his belief that he was divinely appointed to create an army to overthrow the Chinese Government. They are said to have provided the arms needed by his new army in addition to supplying the government he was to overthrow."

"They obviously didn't disclose that they were part of the Opium trade he so strenuously opposed," mused Seraphine.

"I'm sure they didn't," said Grantham.

"Relative to the *Octavius*," interjected Doyle. "You believe the ship was carrying cargo belonging to the Hong's Heavenly Way?"

"I believe the presence of their symbol on the cargo indicates their ownership. However, I concede that their destination to Europe is still a bit of a puzzle," said Grantham with a shrug. "Either the cult, or the Banking Alliance, had an ultimate aim we're not seeing."

"Though their ultimate plan is unclear, we know that the *Octavius'* captain *did* reference Hong himself under the moniker *My King*. So, we have a solid motivation for him attempting the

188

Northwest Passage. Only that kind of cult fervor would convince him that he was divinely equipped to make it."

"All for a cargo of opium?" inquired Seraphine. "That seems to be a weak link in our reasoning."

"Regarding the cargo, I believe it contains something other than Opium," said Grantham. "Did you actually see the cargo, Doyle?"

"No. Moore, the storekeeper, mentioned that it included cases, barrels and sacks of some botanical."

"So, for all you know, the cargo was something else entirely. Barrels and cases are more commonly associated with gun powder and rifles. If the Banking Alliance is involved, the cargo must contain arms - guns easily identified as Chinese and linked to the cult. A remnant of the Heavenly Way must have survived and still retains a link to the Banking Alliance."

"Neither I, nor my druid friends, have ever heard of the Heavenly Way. I assume the remnant died with the *Octavius*," said Seraphine.

"I likewise assume they're gone. However, the Banking Alliance still exists and has greater benefit of the cargo if they make people believe that the cult is also still in existence. They can then push the idea that a Chinese enemy is alive and well, one that cannot be easily dispelled. There's no better enemy than a mysterious cult responsible for 70 million deaths. Such a group would never logically lead back to them."

"If there's no members left, who could they employ to use the arms?" asked Seraphine.

"Members would be convenient, but not entirely necessary. It seems that they're attempting to recruit your druid friends which would be their preferred choice. However, many wars have been started by some act of violence blamed on a particular group, but the actual culprit never formally identified. In the case of the Spanish American War, the event triggering the conflict was the *USS Main* blowing-up in Havana, Cuba. The Spanish denied any involvement to no avail.   All one needs is to employ some henchman to blow-up a key national institution like Westminster Abbey and leave Chinese guns with the mark of the The Way as evidence."

They sat in silence while everyone processed the information. Then Doyle decided to share his fear. "This all seems very logical, but I've been humiliated before in an event that seemed equally logical. This conjecture involving a *conspiracy* involving a *Swiss* group and a forlorn *cult* is equally fanciful on the face of it. How can we prove all of this?"

"Lets think about that," said Grantham. "How would you retrieve the *Octavius?* You mentioned it's deep in the Arctic near Baffin Island. I researched Baffin Island and was surprised to see it spans almost two hundred thousand square miles. That makes it four times larger than all of England. That's a lot of coastline."

"The Banking Alliance would need the exact location including longitude and latitude provided by Captain Garret in his report to the Admiralty," replied Doyle.

"Can you trace the report submitted to the Admiralty to see if the Banking Alliance reviewed it? That would prove some link to the Banking Alliance," observed Seraphine.

"I know that the Admiralty has a very formal process for requesting documents and records of each request. Let me wire a friend at the admiralty and see what he can retrieve about the report," said Doyle.

190

"The Banking Alliance would also need a ship to travel there and retrieve the cargo," continued Grantham. "It's unfortunate that the *Herald* is being scrapped..."

As soon as he said it, all three arrived at the same idea.

"Do we know for sure it's being scrapped?"asked Seraphine.

"I never had cause to verify it," confirmed Doyle. "All I was told was that £100 would be paid to the former crew by the new owners on selling it for parts."

"You need to verify with the scrapyard that the *Herald* is slated for demolition," said Grantham. "If the Banking Alliance is contracting with the new owner and planning to put out to sea again, they can confirm that it's not slated for immediate demolition. That would bring us one step closer to validating our theory."

The three exchanged a few more thoughts and confirmed the plan before Doyle and Seraphine bid their goodbye to the seminary.

As they rode the carriage back to the Whitby, Doyle turned to Seraphine. "When Silas came to me, he said his symptoms began after being confused in *Herald's* gun locker. If our theory is correct, its possible that Chinese guns was brought back that he couldn't identify. In that case, the killer had to silence him before he exposed their plans."

"I suppose, they reinforced his confusion by giving him drugs." mused Seraphine.

"Those same drugs played the groundwork for his death," affirmed Doyle.

"Thank you, Doyle," said Seraphine placing her head on his shoulder. "We're getting closer."

Chapter
Inquiry to the Admiralty

The soft clatter of horse-drawn carriages echoed off the stone buildings as Doyle and Seraphine made their way to the telegraph office. They soon entered a squat brick building with a neatly painted wooden sign reading *Postal & Telegraph Service*. On entering, they found the inside dimly lit by a single gas lamp. Wooden counters, worn smooth by years of use, divided the room, and the faint ticking of the telegraph machine created a steady rhythm in the background.

Doyle removed his hat and stepped forward, followed closely by Seraphine, whose eyes darted around the room as though searching for unseen threats. A bespectacled clerk, thin and pale with ink-stained fingers, looked up from his station with a practiced politeness.

"Good morning," Doyle said, placing a few shillings on the counter. "I need to send a wire to the Admiralty in London. Urgent."

The clerk nodded, sliding a form and pencil toward him. "Please write your message here, sir. Keep it brief; the rate is per word."

Doyle wrote a short message to his friend Captain Forsythe at the Admiralty requesting information on the *Octavius* file and slid the form back across the counter. The clerk scanned it, adjusted his glasses, and turned to the telegraph machine. He tapped out the message in sharp, deliberate bursts, each click of the keys echoing through the room like a tiny hammer strike.

Seraphine leaned closer to Doyle, her voice low. "Do you think he'll have the opportunity to act on this quickly? Or could it become buried in bureaucracy even before your friend receives it?"

"I believe it will be acted upon quickly," Doyle replied, his jaw set. "The Admiralty isn't in the habit of ignoring telegrams. I assume most involve ship movements and potential loss of life at sea."

The clerk turned back, placing a receipt on the counter. "Your message has been sent, sir. Is there anything else?"

"Not at the moment," Doyle said, tipping his hat. He gestured to Seraphine, and together, they left the office. Outside, the streets had grown livelier. Doyle and Seraphine walked briskly toward the nearby railway ticket office, their boots clicking sharply against the cobblestones. The railroad was a more public friendly affair, with large glass windows and a brass-framed clock hanging above the door. Inside, polished wooden benches lined the walls, and a long counter stretched across the far side of the room. Behind it, a man in a neatly pressed uniform stood ready to assist, his mustache curled upward at the edges in the latest fashion.

Doyle approached first opening, removing his gloves and setting them on the counter. "Two tickets to Bristol, please. Second class."

The clerk nodded, flipping through a ledger. "Next train departs in forty minutes, sir. That'll be five shillings."

Doyle counted out the coins and placed them on the counter. The clerk slid two tickets, each stamped with the railway company's crest and the departure time. "Platform three...be sure to board at least five minutes before departure."

Doyle pocketed the tickets and turned to Seraphine who had been surveying the station

"We'll have time for a cup of tea and crumpets before we leave," he said. "I suspect we'll need the energy."

Seraphine nodded, her expression softening slightly. "Good. Tea is always appreciated."

They walked across the station's bustling forecourt to a small tearoom tucked into the corner. Inside, the air was warm and fragrant, filled with the comforting aroma of steeping tea leaves and freshly baked scones. As they sat at a table near the window, Seraphine turned to Doyle, her voice quiet but firm. "Do you expect much from the wire to the admiralty?"

Doyle sipped his tea thoughtfully before answering. "I asked that Forsythe confirm the contents of the file in addition to information on the requestor including dates and contact information. If the Banking Alliance obtained the information, we'll know who they're working with and when they started."

"If we don't receive any information from your friend in-time, at least we'll have our findings from the scrapyard in Bristol. If the Herald isn't slated for destruction, we're one step closer to finding a link to the Banking Alliance."

The train's whistle cut through the air, and the carriage jolted forward. Doyle settled into his seat, steeling himself for what lay ahead.

They arrived at their destination three hours later to a scene of organized chaos. The scrapyard sprawled out before them, a maze of ships in various stages of disassembly. The air was thick with the sounds of hammers striking metal and the sharp clang of heavy machinery. The scent of saltwater mixed with the earthy aroma of wet wood filled the air, an intoxicating reminder of the sea.

As they walked through the yard, Doyle's eyes scanned the area, taking in the remnants of ships stripped bare. Some vessels stood like skeletons, their hulls exposed, while others were little more than heaps of timber. He noticed the absence of masts and rigging; the remnants of sailing ships were reduced to their essential parts, waiting to be transformed into something new.

They approached the office of the scrapyard's manager, a burly man with a weathered face, indicative of years spent working among the ships. The man leaned against the doorframe, crossing his arms as he regarded them with a mixture of curiosity and skepticism

"Good morning," Doyle said with a smile. "We're here to inquire about a ship called the *Herald*."

The owner raised an eyebrow. "*Herald*? I don't have a ship by that name scheduled for scrapping." His voice was gruff, yet there was an underlying note of professionalism. "We handle a lot of vessels around here, but if it's not on the list, it's not coming here."

Doyle pressed further. "Can you check the list for sure?"

The man entered a little office that seemed as chaotic as the shipyard. However, he deftly retrieved a paper from within a pile on the desk and reviewed.

"Like I said, no *Herald*," he declared.

"We're under the impression that it's arriving in a few days and the proceeds of the sale will be distributed at that time. Is it too far in advance for it to be on your list?" asked Seraphine.

The manager shook his head as if trying to remain patient. "A ship gets on my list a fair amount of time before it makes it here - way back at the beginning stages of its preparation for towing. Where it is and what condition is it in? Are the masts and rigging still on it?"

"Its moored in Whitby. Its in good condition and the masts are there and still holding canvas," responded Doyle.

"That ship ain't going to scrap anytime soon. First, the ship must be stripped of its masts and rigging. That's a crucial part of the process; we can't have those sticking out when it gets towed here. Then, the hull is inspected, and any hazardous materials and any cargo are removed. Only then can it be safely towed here for dismantling. That takes several weeks. If your *Herald* ain't even begun to be stripped, it ain't coming here or having any money given for it. Are you sure it's being scrapped? It sounds like it may put out to sea soon."

"It may. Thank you for your time," Doyle said, feeling a mix of gratitude and urgency. They left and boarded the next train back to Whitby and the *Herald*.

The train rumbled along the tracks, the rhythmic clatter of wheels against steel created a soothing background, but it did little to ease the tension between Doyle and Seraphine. They settled into their seats, the weight of their discoveries from the scrapyard pressing heavily on their minds.

"So, the *Herald* is probably going out to sea again..." said Seraphine. "If so, how would the crew get paid £100?"

"It's baffling, isn't it? Why would the captain say everyone is getting paid when the ship obviously isn't being scrapped?" asked Doyle.

"Maybe he doesn't know. Either way, somebody wanted to gather the crew together one more time. What was their real motive?" asked Seraphine frustrated. "They certainly didn't care to solve the deaths in the Arctic."

"Given that two crew have died under mysterious circumstances, I can only assume that gathering the crew is part of the larger plan. Could it be that they need the crew dead?"

"Why would they need everyone dead?"

"That's the question, isn't it…"

Chapter
Admiralty Findings

On the return to Whitby, Doyle was surprised to have a response from the admiralty waiting at the telegraph office.

"How did your friend research it so fast?" Seraphine asked. "I could understand determining who may have retrieved the document quickly, but you asked him to review it also. I assume that would take some additional time."

Doyle handed her the telegram. "It will make more sense when you read it."

To: A. C. Doyle
Fr: Captain Forsythe
Regarding: Octavius

I confirm there was no report filed with admiralty for sail vessel Octavius.

Forsythe

"So, no file was ever delivered and Garret lied?" Seraphine said incredulously.

"That's the logical conclusion. I think it's now clear that he lied twice. Firstly, he deceived us about the *Herald* being sold for scrap. Secondly, he lied about the admiralty being aware of the very existence of the *Octavius*. The only other alternative is that someone removed the file and managed to edit all documentation regarding its entry in the archives index and submission logs. That same person, or group, convinced Garret that the ship was being sold for scrap."

"Wait," said Seraphine. "Let's look at each development separately. Could anyone remove the *Octavius* report without leaving some sort of trail?"

"I don't see how, the Admiralty's log entries and index are handwritten in ledgers with an ink pen. It's possible to line-out an entry with a pen, but the document and its receipt would still be visible under the scribbled line. Medical records operate under a similar principle to eliminate manipulation after a procedure or diagnosis."

"Could there be some conspiracy in the admiralty that inserted new pages that appeared unaltered?" Seraphine asked. "In my profession, the impossible is done everyday with the simplest tricks."

"I suppose that's possible," agreed Doyle. "However, I believe it would require several people to be in on the deception given the controls on government documents."

"So, it's possible, but unlikely. That leaves the question regarding Garret being duped that the *Herald* was being sold for scrap. That still seems plausible. Who is the owner?"

"I don't know. It wasn't relevant up to this time. I assume it's possible that the owner, whoever it is, could tell Garret that the ship was being retired for scrap. It's entirely likely given its age."

They sat in silence for another minute. Then, Doyle exhaled deeply and made a small confession. "Try as I might, I don't have the *all seeing* powers of my Holmes creation. So, lets assume that Garret never submitted the *Octavius'* report *and* lied about the *Herald* being sent to the scrapyard. Now, we must deduce why he did it?"

"I suppose the reason could involve the *Octavius* and its cargo, or the death of Silas, or both. If it's regarding the *Octavius'* cargo, the motive would be profit. If it was the death of Silas, it would be to cover his guilt, or the protection of another," concluded Seraphine.

Doyle nodded his head. "If there were arms aboard, he could have attempted to find a buyer and subsequently discovered the Banking Alliance. We know that Garret is involved somehow, because he saw the cargo when he went back for Moore."

"We also have no proof that the Banking Alliance is involved. I refuse for you to be humiliated again by another Cottingley Fairies' incident. How can we get proof now that neither the Admiralty nor the scrapyard could provide us any documentation linking them?"

"I don't know. We can't interrogate Garret because he's lied before. Questioning the crew hasn't yielded anything we didn't already know. The seance is the only thing that triggered a strong response and we're running out of time. Whatever the plan, we assume it involves the killer striking again. That's the one part of the plan that seems evident from the deaths so far."

"Agreed," said Seraphine nodding her head. "One last seance is the answer. However, this time, we'll combine our skills to make quite a spectacle. I think's its our last chance, regardless of the danger."

Chapter
Final Seance

The lights in the galley were extinguished with a single candle casting shadows that extended into darkness beyond the ship's walls. The room seemed empty despite it's small size with only four participants remaining - Garret, Li, Moore and Baines.

Seraphine entered, her steps slow and deliberate, her eyes dark with intent. She raised a hand to silence the murmurs that ran through the four remaining crew gathered around the table, their faces flickering in the candlelight.

"Gentlemen," she began, her voice low and resonant. "Tonight, I will call our adventure to a close. We will call forth the spirits of those lost." She let the words linger as the shadows danced behind her.

"Where's Doyle?" Garret asked.

"Doyle," she said after a pause for effect, "is unable to join us due to the unfortunate media from the Cottingley Ferry incident. He came to realize that all answers lie in the spirit world alone and there is no place for his earthly investigation. For his reputation's sake, he returned to London."

"But this nightmare will end tonight," said Garret addressing the remaining crew. "Yer obligation'll be finished."

The men exchanged glances, unsure if they believed either of them, but it hardly mattered. Their attention clung to Seraphine as she took her place at the head of the table. She shut her eyes and lifted her hands. Her voice softened as she began to call on the spirit world.

The first sign of Silas was a faint shimmer in the corner of the galley, a ghostly outline that seemed to grow clearer with each word that escaped Seraphine's lips. Shadows crawled up the walls, and an echo of raking chains clanked from somewhere below. The men shifted nervously, glancing toward the closed doors, where the sounds grew louder, as if someone was dragging heavy iron on the deck.

The form of Silas grew clearer, taking on color and texture, appearing more solid than ever before. His eyes glistened with a sadness that chilled them all, but his face was drawn with a clarity that none could deny. It was as if he had crossed back from death to stand among them once more.

"Silas," Seraphine whispered, her voice steady. "You've come to us again. Tell us—tell these men who took your life."

Silas's gaze seemed to stare at each crew member before speaking through Seraphine. "I was murdered by the same hand that ended the lives of Winthrop and MacLeod. The same darkness, corrupt and ruthless."

A murmur ran between the four. Two cursed under their breaths and stared straight at Silas. Two others cast wary glances looking for others in their midst.

Silas's form wavered, and the sounds of raking chains grew louder. Shadows moved over the walls, twisting and curling like hands reaching out for something just beyond reach. "*Herald* will sail again," Silas said again, channeled through Seraphine, "but it will not see the scrapyard. The ship will carry death, blood, and ruin. This vessel has become a pawn, its fate bound to the whims of men who care nothing for your lives."

The room was filled with moaning sounds. "The spirits are increasingly restless." Silas continued louder now, filled with an urgency that had the men leaning forward in spite of themselves. "They know evil plans are in motion. Evil men seek to profit from mass death, to turn nations against each other. They will plunge the world into chaos, all to line their pockets and feed their greed."

Silas's form flickered, as though a wind had blown through him, but steadied.

"Who are these men?" Li asked.

Before Silas could answer, a metallic clicking like the cocking of a gun could be heard, causing the men to stir. The candle likewise went out, and for a moment, darkness engulfed the room with movement detected. The gas lights came back on - bathing the galley in harsh, glaring light.

Blocking the doorway was Garret, flanked by Moore and a third man they didn't recognize—a tall figure with cold, calculating eyes and an air of wealth and entitlement. His gaze swept the room with disdain.

"Quite the show, Doyle," Garret sneered, his hand restin' easy on the revolver at his hip. "Step out now, or I'll put a bullet in yer lady friend..."

Doyle emerged from behind a wall holding a chain. Moore grinned, his eyes gleaming with something close to amusement.

The stranger stepped forward, his voice low but chillingly clear. "I think it's time we ended this nonsense," he said with a Swiss accent. He gestured to Moore to take a new position at the other exit leading to the kitchen.

"What's happening?" Baines exclaimed.

"They're about to explain it," said Doyle. "We deserve that much."

Garret nodded, crossing his arms. "We're goin' to fetch the cargo from the *Octavius*. Cases o' rifles, pistols, and gunpowder— the sort that'll make a real splash."

"They won't understand," said Doyle angrily. "Go back to the beginning and explain it all."

Garret glanced at the Swiss man who nodded his ascent. "Banes an' I found that the *Octavius'* cargo was full o' guns, munitions, an' a few botanicals. We brought back two rifles after settin' the tow to Baffin Island as a sample fer potential buyers. Thought no one noticed 'til Doyle mentioned not recallin' us leavin' the Herald with 'em. I covered it by sayin' otherwise, but Silas found them strange weapons in the gun locker. I told 'im he was confused, an' slipped some opium from Moore's private stock in his tobacco to keep the lie runnin'. After he had a word with Doyle, he said the symptoms started when he went near the gun locker, but he didn't give enough detail to make Doyle put the pieces together. But we knew if Silas came 'round, he'd spill enough to make Doyle connect the dots."

Moore interjected, "It was my idea to pretend to replicate Silas symptoms and blame it on the *Octavius* curse. I made a show of being delirious and was taken to Doyle's cabin to distract him while Garret slipped Silas more of my opium mixture in his tobacco. The next day, Silas smoked again and went into a wild state. While everyone was looking for him, I found him first and ended him. With him, went the secret of the guns."

"You killed a dear, innocent man," said Seraphine with intense hatred in here eyes. A stunned silence followed.

"Why bring us all back here?" asked Doyle bringing the conversation back to Garret fearing that Seraphine might be shot if she flew into a rage at Moore.

"Moore asked some o' his less reputable contacts, tryin' ta find a buyer, but got nowhere. Nobody wanted the stuff. The

206

Chinese guns and powder weren't worth the trouble o' mountin' an expedition ta haul 'em off the *Octavius*. So, we carried on with our lives an' let it be."

"How did the Banking Alliance learn about it?" asked Doyle.

"Ahh...so you know our name, Dr. Doyle," interjected the Swiss man. "Our suspicions that you would discover our little plot were correct. Not-to-worry, you'll be dealt with along with the rest."

Doyle fought the urge to fly at him and responded, "You still didn't answer my question..."

"There has been an unfortunate period of peace that's cutting into our profits. We sought ways to replicate our biggest money maker, the Opium War. We were thrilled to happen upon a ghost story involving the very cult that made our organization that much richer and two men attempting to sell their weapons. We investigated further and found Moore and Garret. The rest of the plan you obviously figured out based on your little theatrics" he said gesturing to Seraphine.

"*We* know your plan, but please elaborate for Li and Banes. Since you're obviously going to kill us all, you owe it to them," said Doyle with disgust.

The man became agitated, but complied with a grossly abbreviated description directed at the two men. "You see, gentlemen, the plan is simple. We'll retrieve the cargo with the *Herald and* bring it back to England. We recruit just enough disenfranchised spiritualists, like druids, to make it seem that the cult owning the weapons on the *Octavius* is still in existence. We'll use hired henchmen to conduct a few well-placed attacks on notable locations—Parliament or Westminster Abbey. We then direct authorities, anomalously of course, to a few of our new members of The Way. We'll plant weapons with the Way's Chinese symbols on their properties that the authorities will be sure to find. All eyes will turn to China and our untraceable cult. We'll ply politicians in the East *and* the West with enough fear to start a war. Then we'll start our profits flowing again by supplying both sides with money and weapons. With luck, we can even own the opium trade again."

"What about me?" Seraphine interjected. "Why invite me to do a seance, did you know I was Silas sister?"

"You're his sister..." exclaimed the man with genuine surprise and new interest. "How terribly convenient - one less loose end. All we knew was that Doyle had become rich due to his books and wouldn't come here for money. However, we read about his little escapades with the Cottingley Fairies. So, the idea was formed to use a medium and his interest in spirits to create an event to solve the mystery that's plagued him since his time on the *Herald*.You were selected because you seemed to have no family and appeared from nowhere. In other words, you wouldn't be missed after your untimely death with the others."

"What we didn't count on..." interjected Garret. "Was you two bein' so good at solvin' the mystery. Shoulda killed ye after the first seance. How were we to know Madame Seraphine would make such a ruckus, seemin' to bring Silas back?"

"That was inconvenient," agreed the Swiss man. "Now it appears we must deal with other loose ends including a druidic bookseller, a chemist and a priest."

The man pulled a silver whistle from his pocket, blowing a shrill, piercing note that echoed through the room. They waited, a sense of dread filling the room as footsteps thundered above, growing louder as the men summoned to finish the job approached. But instead of the stranger's henchmen, a different sound filled the hall—a rush of boots, the clinking of rifles, and the barked orders of a British Naval Officer. The galley door burst open, revealing a detachment of armed men in dark uniforms. The officer stepped forward, his face resolute, his gaze sweeping over the conspirators with steely disdain.

"Dr. Doyle, the Admiralty sends its appreciation for your timely message." He turned to Garret, Moore, and the stranger, his expression cold. "And *thank you* gentleman for the lengthy confession."

Chapter
Royal Navy

Garret, Moore, and their associates were marched off the *Herald* and onto the waiting navy sloop. The four survivors stood on the deck, watching the scene unfold in silence. The gray mist had begun to lift as the morning sun peeked out over the harbor. Once the last of the prisoners disappeared below the sloop's deck, Doyle turned to Mr. Li with a thoughtful expression.

"Mr. Li," he began, choosing his words carefully, "I must admit, that I look liberties searching your things after suspecting you of working with Garret. I found a photograph of a family with you in a naval uniform which confused me about your past. So, when you had a reaction to seeing the cult's symbol, I thought your past caused some involvement. I apologize."

Li's expression became somber, but he did not look offended. Instead, he seemed appreciative.

"I understand, Dr. Doyle," he said, his English slow and deliberate. "You see many things that… do not look good. But… it is not what it look."

Doyle nodded, sensing there was more. "If you're willing, I'd like to understand. There's clearly more to your story, and we'd like to hear it, if you're willing."

Li sighed, looking out toward the misty sea, his voice lowered with old grief. "That mark—the mark of that cult—it bring back… bad memories." He paused, gathering his thoughts. "Long time ago, I was… naval officer in the Chinese Imperial Navy fighting British during Opium War."

Li stopped and took a slow breath, eyes distant trying to contain his emotions. "After war, I go home. My… family, my village…" His voice caught, and he struggled to continue, "… all gone. Burned, destroyed. No one left. My wife, my daughters… they die when village… taken by cult's war."

A silence settled between them as the weight of his words hung in the air. Seraphine reached out and gently touched Li's shoulder, a quiet gesture of empathy.

Li went on. "I know that British not kill family. It was emperor's soldiers trying to eliminate Heavenly Way. I learned that Heavenly Way started war to stop opium trade and remove government. Opium was evil, but bringing on execution to innocent people not involved in movement even worse."

Doyle listened, understanding dawning on him. "So you left China?"

Li nodded slowly, a bitter smile crossing his lips. "I leave, yes. Too much sadness. Too many ghosts. Could not return to serve Emperor when Chinese Imperial Army killed my family." Li's voice grew faint and he stopped to collect himself. "I find work on whaling ship, cook for men. Hard work, but no one ask about past. I think… maybe I forget. Then, on *Herald,* we see *Octavius*. I see mark on ship, that old mark, nightmare come back." He closed his eyes briefly, collecting himself. "But then we leave it behind, and I think it gone. Like demon."

Doyle studied him carefully. "And when Silas died…?"

Li shook his head, a resolute expression on his face. "I know then, this not cult's doing. Cult—they hate opium. I know crew hide something, but not for me. I just cook."

There was a long silence, then eyes turned to Banes.

"I understand your hurt more than anyone, Mr. Li" said Baines. "When asked, I always said I was on ships in the spice

212

trade. But that wasn't exactly true. I worked in the opium trade and saw how it wiped-out a generation of Chinese. I couldn't handle being a part of that anymore. I decided to ply my trade as a sailmaker on whaling ships as far from China as possible. I apologize for being evasive when you asked about that part of my past, Doyle."

"I'm sorry for bringing back old memories," said Doyle extending his hand to both men.

Li accepted his hand, nodding slowly. "No need sorry, Dr. Doyle. Dark times… they make us see ghosts, even when there no ghosts."

Baines turned to Madame Seraphine and said, "Perhaps we can now release our ghosts including your brother. His killer will finally hang."

Seraphine simply nodded. After a moment, she said to Doyle, "The thing I don't understand is how your dream included a warning from the *Octavius* crew about The Way. We hadn't heard of the cult until later and it shouldn't have appeared in a nightmare. Do you think they were truly trying to ward you from the other side?"

Doyle just shrugged. "Perhaps we can explore that and more together, my dear…"

She smiled, "I'd like that."

After a while, the sun rose higher, casting a warm light over the deck. For the first time since they'd set foot on the *Herald*, the darkness that had clung to the ship seemed to lift, replaced by a quiet, newfound peace.

213

Appendix A
Octavius

Octavius **Myth and Its Discovery of the Northwest Passage**
The *Octavius* is one of the most enduring maritime legends of the 18th century. Allegedly, the derelict ship was found adrift in the Arctic with its entire crew frozen. The captain was said to be still seated frozen at his desk while penning the ship's log. The log allegedly indicated that the ship had been locked in ice near Point Barrow, Alaska. A decade later, the derelict was found on the other side of the frozen Northwest Passage passage near Greenland. That position made the derelict the first ship to traverse the passage. The myth has been embellished and retold over time, in a testament to maritime exploration.

Earliest References to the *Octavius*
The *Octavius* legend first gained prominence in 1775, when the whaling ship *Herald* was reputed to encounter the vessel near Greenland. According to accounts, the *Herald*'s crew boarded the abandoned ship and discovered its frozen crew, eerily preserved by the Arctic cold. This discovery suggested that the *Octavius* had been trapped in the ice after successfully navigating the Northwest Passage, drifting aimlessly ever since. However, no primary source from the *Herald* or its crew has ever been verified, and most accounts of the *Octavius* story come from later retellings. For a practical matter, the probability that a wooden ship could drift intact for over a decade through intermittent ice is highly unlikely. Ice would have crushed the vessel long before it reached Greenland.

215

Evolution of the *Octavius* Myth

Over the centuries, the *Octavius* legend has evolved, incorporating new details and interpretations. The earliest printed reference was traced to a Philadelphia newspaper, *The Ariel: A Literary and Critical Gazette in 1828*. In that version there was no mention of the Northwest Passage, and the derelict ship remained nameless. Subsequent retellings embellished the original legend - added the ship name *Octavius* and location in the Northwest Passage.

Origins of the Northwest Passage

Prior to the development of the Panama Canal, ships were forced to travel around The Horn at great peril. The Horn, also known as Cape Horn, is the southernmost tip of South America at the confluence of the Atlantic and Pacific Oceans. Sailing around Cape Horn continues to be a dangerous route due to extreme winds, massive waves, and icebergs.

Given the tremendous length and danger associated with The Horn, 17th century European explorers began searching for a sea route connecting the Atlantic and Pacific Oceans through the Arctic. The discovery of such a route would dramatically lower the cost of trade with the Orient and eliminate the need to travel around the dangerous waters of The Horn. Expeditions were mounted by leading explorers including John Cabot, Martin Frobisher, and others - most ending in disaster. The Franklin Expedition seeking the Northwest Passage was launched in 1845 but ended in tragedy when both ships, HMS *Erebus* and HMS *Terror*, became icebound, and all 129 crew members perished. Researchers discovered the wreck of *Erebus* in 2014 and *Terror* in 2016, shedding light on the crew's fate through preserved artifacts and skeletal remains.The discovery of the ships and crew resurrected popularity of the *Octavius* myth in social media.

Modern exploration confirmed the existence of the Northwest Passage in the early 20th century when Norwegian explorer Roald Amundsen successfully navigated the waterway between 1903 and 1906. However, returning Arctic ice made the route impractical. In recent decades, climate change has caused significant Arctic ice loss, allowing the passage to thaw during summer months and become temporarily navigable. The route refreezes in the winter, making year-round travel impossible. Other factors complicating it's use include concerns about safety, environmental impacts, and geopolitical tensions over Arctic sovereignty.

Modern tourists can sail over the now thawed North Pole on cruises during the summer months when seasonal melting makes the region slightly navigable.

Appendix B
Arthur Conan Doyle

The Life of Medicine, Whaling, and Spiritualism
Doyle (1859–1930) is best known as the creator of Holmes and Watson, but his life was far more varied and complex than commonly known. These diverse experiences as a physician, adventurer, and spiritualist experiences shaped his career and worldview. Experiences relevant to this book included the time at medical school, position on a whaling ship and involvement in the Cottingley Fairies controversy.

Early Life and Medical School
Doyle was born on May 22, 1859, in Edinburgh, Scotland, into a devoutly Catholic family. Though his childhood was overshadowed by his father's struggles with alcoholism and mental health, Doyle excelled in academics. In 1876, at the age of 17, he enrolled at the University of Edinburgh to study medicine. During his medical training, Doyle studied under renowned professors, including Dr. Joseph Bell, a surgeon whose keen observational skills and deductive reasoning inspired the character of Holmes. Bell's ability to deduce patients' occupations, habits, and ailments through observation left a lasting impression on Doyle. This fascination with deduction and logic later became the cornerstone of his detective fiction. To support his education, Doyle worked as a ship's doctor and harpooner during his breaks from university. One such voyage in 1880 took him aboard the whaling ship *Hope*, bound for the Arctic.

Adventures on the *Hope*

As the ship's medical officer, Doyle was responsible for the health and well-being of the crew, many of whom faced injuries and illnesses during the dangerous Arctic whaling expedition. Doyle embraced the rough, adventurous life at sea, finding it both physically demanding and intellectually stimulating. The harsh beauty of the Arctic landscape left a vivid impression on Doyle, and he recorded his experiences in a detailed journal. These notes, filled with observations about the icy wilderness, the camaraderie of the crew, and the brutal reality of whaling, later inspired his adventure writing. The trip also introduced Doyle to the concept of courage in the face of adversity, a recurring theme throughout his literary and personal life.

The Birth of Holmes

After earning his medical degree in 1881, Doyle began a struggling medical practice in Southsea, England. While waiting for patients, he began writing stories to supplement his income. In 1887, his first novel featuring Holmes, *A Study in Scarlet*, was published. The Watson character drew heavily from Doyle's medical school experiences. The character of Holmes was partially built from Dr. Joseph Bell's deductive methods. Doyle initially planned to name his famous detective "Sherringford Holmes." His mother found the name to be weak and suggested that he adopt the name of a childhood friend, "Sherlock." The change gave the character a sharper, more distinctive identity, which helped solidify his place in literary history. The success of the detective stories brought Doyle fame and financial stability, allowing him to pursue other interests beyond writing. Doyle was knighted in 1902 for his work with a field hospital in Bloemfontein, South Africa, and other services during the South African (Boer) War. His knighthood wasn't conferred until two years after this fictional story took place. As a result, this title is not mentioned within the context of this book.

The Cottingley Fairies Controversy

In 1917, Doyle became embroiled in one of the most peculiar episodes of his life: the Cottingley Fairies controversy. Two young cousins in Yorkshire, Frances Griffiths and Elsie Wright, claimed to have photographed fairies near their home. The photographs, showing small, winged figures in natural settings, captivated the public and divided opinion between believers and skeptics. Doyle, already deeply interested in spiritualism and the supernatural, embraced the photographs as evidence of an unseen world. He published an article in *The Strand Magazine* and later a book, *The Coming of the Fairies* (1922), defending the images' authenticity. Critics derided Doyle's credulity, but his defense of the fairies reflected his broader belief in the existence of mystical phenomena. Decades later, the cousins admitted to faking the photographs using cardboard cutouts.

The Cottingley Fairies incident took place almost 20 after the timeframe of this fictional story. However, given that it was integral to the plot, editorial license was used to bring the date of the event forward by two decades.

Doyle and Mysticism

Doyle's interest in mysticism began in the late 1880s, but it became a central passion after the deaths of his son Kingsley and others after World War I. The grieving Doyle turned to mysticism to seek solace and communication with the lost loved-ones through mediums. Doyle became one of spiritualism's most prominent advocates, traveling the world to lecture on its merits. He wrote extensively on the subject, including *The New Revelation* (1918) and *The History of Spiritualism* (1926). He attended seances and championed the work of mediums, believing that spiritualism offered proof of life after death. His advocacy attracted both followers and harsh critics. Scientists and skeptics accused Doyle of gullibility, arguing that mediums were frauds that exploited the bereaved. Nevertheless, Doyle remained steadfast in his belief, viewing spiritualism as both a science and a religion.

Friendship and Falling Out with Harry Houdini

One of the most intriguing chapters in Doyle's life was his friendship with the world-famous magician, Harry Houdini. The two men initially bonded over their shared fascination with the supernatural. Houdini, while skeptical of spiritualism, admired Doyle's intellect and sincerity. In return, while Doyle admired Houdini's apparent otherworldly abilities. However, their friendship soured due to their opposing views on mysticism. Houdini was a staunch skeptic who devoted much of his career to debunking fraudulent mediums. He often exposed their tricks in public demonstrations. Doyle, for his part, was convinced that Houdini possessed genuine paranormal abilities based on his theatrical performances. This belief continued despite Houdini's insistence that his miraculous feats were purely illusions. The breaking point came when Doyle's wife, Jean, conducted a seance to contact Houdini's deceased mother. Houdini was deeply offended by the seance's fraudulent nature and publicly criticized the spiritualism. Their disagreement escalated and the two became bitter enemies.

Later Years and Legacy

Doyle continued to write and advocate for the mysticism until his death. In his later years, he grew increasingly frustrated with the public's focus on Holmes. He attempted to kill the character through a showdown with the detective's arch enemy in 1893. However, public pressure forced Holme's revival in subsequent stories. Doyle's commitment to mysticism overshadowed his literary accomplishments in his final years.

He passed away on July 7, 1930, at his home in Crowborough, England, reportedly calling out to his wife. Today, Doyle is celebrated as one of the greatest writers of detective fiction, but his life reflects a deeper complexity.

Appendix C
The Heavenly Way

The Taiping Rebellion and the Heavenly Way

The Taiping Rebellion (1850–1864) was one of the bloodiest conflicts in world history, costing an estimated 50 -70 million lives. Led by Hong Xiuquan, the rebellion sought to overthrow the Qing Dynasty and establish the Heavenly Kingdom, a theocratic state driven by radical religious and social reforms. The rebellion's roots are found at Thistle Mountain where its spiritual leader's claim to divinity through a cult called the "Heavenly Way," grew from devastation of the Opium Wars.

Socio-Economic Turmoil and the Opium Wars

The Taiping Rebellion emerged against a backdrop of widespread suffering and unrest in mid-19th-century China. The Qing Dynasty, already weakened by internal corruption, faced growing foreign pressure following its defeat in the First Opium War (1839–1842). The Treaty of Nanking, which ended the war, imposed severe reparations on China, ceded Hong Kong to Britain, and opened several Chinese ports to foreign trade. This humiliation, coupled with the British opium trade's ongoing devastation of China's economy and society, left many disillusioned with Qing rule.

Opium, introduced by British traders, had become a scourge that drained China of silver and debilitated large swathes of its population. Efforts by Qing officials to suppress the opium trade had failed, leading to the Second Opium War (1856–1860). The resulting social disintegration created fertile ground for rebellion, particularly in impoverished southern regions like Guangxi, where dissatisfaction with the Qing reached a boiling point.

Hong Xiuquan and the Birth of the Taiping Movement

The leader of the Taiping Rebellion, Hong Xiuquan, was born in 1814 in a poor Hakka village in Guangdong province. As a member of the Hakka ethnic group, Hong belonged to a marginalized minority. A failed scholar who repeatedly fell short in the imperial civil service exams, Hong's frustrations with the Confucian-dominated social order grew over time.

In 1837, after one such failure, Hong experienced a series of visions that he later interpreted as divine revelations. Years later, after reading Christian missionary tracts distributed by Westerners, Hong came to believe he was the younger brother of Jesus Christ, chosen by God to save China from demonic forces—chief among them, the Qing rulers.

By the 1840s, Hong had begun to gather followers in southern China, preaching his altered version of Christianity and vision of a Heavenly Kingdom on Earth. He called his movement the "Heavenly Way" and declared that China needed to rid itself of corruption, idolatry, and the oppressive Qing regime.

Thistle Mountain

Thistle Mountain became the cradle of the Taiping movement. There, Hong and his earliest disciples established their base for teachings and military recruitment. The remote, rugged terrain of Thistle Mountain provided both a physical refuge and a symbolic foundation for their mission. Hong preached against opium smoking, gambling, the worship of traditional Chinese deities, and Christian fundamentalism.

The Rebellion's Rise and Connection to the Opium Wars

The British opium trade began in the late18th century after China rebuffed the West's efforts at establishing trade. The China position basically stated that China self produced everything needed and therefore had no desire for British goods. To balance their trade deficit, Britain began exporting Indian opium to China, creating widespread addiction. Opium buyers were forced to to buy British products in exchange for silver. Some United States merchants followed and likewise traded opium acquired from Turkey.

The legacy of the Opium Wars played a pivotal role in the Taiping Rebellion's rise. The wars exposed the Qing Dynasty's inability to protect China from Opium traders. The economic devastation wrought by the opium trade and unequal treaties further fueled resentment among the rural population.

The Taiping movement capitalized on this discontent, portraying the Qing as weak, corrupt, and complicit in China's humiliation. Hong Xiuquan framed the rebellion as a divine mission to cleanse China of foreign influence, including the opium trade. To establish validity, he declared himself God's other son in addition to Jesus Christ.

The Fall of the Taiping Heavenly Kingdom

The Western powers, while critical of the Qing, viewed the Taiping's anti-foreigner and anti-Christian rhetoric as a threat to their interests. After securing concessions from the Qing in the Treaty of Tianjin (1858), These powers provided indirect support to the Qing forces, allowing them to focus on suppressing the rebellion. Hong Xiuquan, the self proclaimed deity and "Heavenly King," reportedly died of illness or suicide during the movement's defeat. The final death tole of his followers and rural Chinese as estimated at 70 million, leaving entire areas devoid of people.

The Chinese Symbol Identifying Heavenly Kingdom Movement

The Chinese symbol employed by the movement incorporated a unique blend of traditional elements, reflecting both their spiritual and philosophical underpinnings. The central symbol featured a depiction of multiple deities or cosmic forces, evoking the principles of polytheism. Above this symbol was a distinct circle, a feature not commonly seen in conventional Chinese religious iconography. This circle, often interpreted as a symbol for unity or singularity, sat atop the polytheism design, suggesting a transcendent force that harmonized with the multiple deities. This addition of the circle spoke to to the Heavenly Way's unusual view of the divine, where individual gods coexisted within a larger single deity.

Appendix D
The Banking Alliance

International Banking Conspiracy Theory

A common conspiracy theory exists where international banking elites under various names including the Council of Foreign Relations and the Trilateral Commission use their wealth and influence to manipulate global politics. It's alleged that these bankers create crises, such as wars and revolution, to destabilize nations. Governments, left financially crippled by these crises, turn to these elites for loans, indebting themselves and surrendering significant policy control.

A key premise of the theory allege that these banking elites actively promote tensions between nations to encourage military spending and the accumulation of debt. They allege that geopolitical rivalries, such as the Cold War between the United States and the Soviet Union, are not accidental but rather orchestrated by the bankers to ensure governments remain reliant on their financial support.

The Russian Revolution and the Role of Lenin

One of the most striking assertions of the theory claim that the Russian Revolution of 1917, which led to the rise of communism, was financed and facilitated by the same banking elites. The cite the fact that Russia's brief democratic government, established after the abdication of Tsar Nicholas II, posed a threat to the global elites because it sought to assert national sovereignty and reduce foreign financial influence. They believe that these banking elites financed Vladimir Lenin and the Bolsheviks to overthrow this democratic government and establishing a communist regime. The end result was two diverse forms of government, communism and democracy, that would be in constant conflict for decades. This conflict would result in an arms race with deficit financing that requires financing.

Counter Argument to an International Banking Conspiracy

The World Bank was created after WWII along with the International Monetary Fund (IMF), with the primary goal of fostering global economic stability and development. The Bank's mission was to provide financial assistance and technical expertise to developing countries for infrastructure projects, poverty reduction, and economic growth. Its creation marked the beginning of a new global financial order, with lender nations—particularly the United States and other Western powers—taking a leading role in organizing and funding development programs. The World Bank's structure was designed to facilitate low interest loans to countries in need, with the aim of stimulating long-term economic development and promoting global peace. The World Bank includes both democratic and communist (or formerly communist) nations as its members.